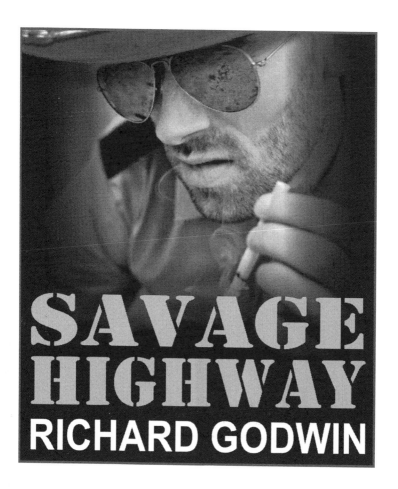

SAVAGE HIGHWAY

RICHARD GODWIN

WILDBLUE
P R E S S

D1594241

WildBluePress.com

SAVAGE HIGHWAY is a work of fiction. Any resemblance to a person, or persons, or historical events is entirely coincidental.

SAVAGE HIGHWAY published by:
WILDBLUE PRESS
1153 Bergen Pkwy Ste I #114
Evergreen, Colorado 80439

978-1-942266-33-4Trade Paperback ISBN
978-1-942266-34-1eBook ISBN

Interior Formatting by Elijah Toten
www.totencreative.com

Book Cover Design Page Godwin

For Page

1.

Midnight.

Beyond the stained window the hissing scar of the highway was deserted. Patty was aching with hunger. The diner was empty apart from the guy in the corner. He'd been eyeing her all night.

'I don't suppose you have a light?' he said, walking over.

'Sure,' Patty said, flicking her Zippo, then snuffing out the brief flame. 'Spare a smoke?'

'Oh *yeah*.'

The waitress bristled past, all swish of starched uniform and the click of over-chewed gum. She looked at them out of the corner of her eye, a slight curl of her lip.

'They call me Jim,' he said. 'You coming?'

Patty followed him outside into the mix of ice cold and diesel fumes. After the initial silence, they started the smokers' chat. Weather, journeys, directions, bitching about this and that, and then he said it. Just like that. No interlude, no buildup. As if he was ordering a burger.

'Last night I killed a man.' He took a deep drag and blew it skywards then turned and looking her right in the eyes. 'A guy got smart. He was nobody, really. I shot him. Twice.'

'That right?'

Silence. And just two burning cigarette ends in the cold and the smog. A truck whizzed by.

'Why you telling me this?' she said.

''Cause there's one thing I always feel like doing after I kill someone.'

'No shit?'

'You look good to me with your dark brown eyes and your long hair. Got a good figure on you. Good ass, too. You're a real brunette bombshell.'

'I ain't gonna sleep with you.'

'I ain't asking you to sleep with me, honey. How old are you anyway?'

'Twenty-six.'

'That right? There's a bad dude out there, in case you ain't heard. He's been chopping women up. Much badder'n old Jim. I don't kill ladies, just fuck 'em.'

'I can look after myself.'

'Heard one woman got her throat opened up. Out here, alone, just her thumb in the air and only her poontang to pay. They call him the maniac trucker, although I hear this guy drives a pickup.'

'Thanks for the smoke,' she said, walking back in.

Inside, the waitress stared at her from behind the counter, hands on her hips. Just another anonymous small-town judge. Patty watched as she went out back. She felt weak as Jim walked in, laughing, almost dancing across the diner to where she sat.

'Come on, we can do it in the john,' he said.

'What makes you think you can buy me?'

'I know desperation when I see it.'

The smell of pizza drifted across the air.

'How much you got?'

'I knew you were a pickup. I reckon you're worth a hundred.'

'Hundred and fifty.'

'Done.'

He peeled a stack of tens out of his wallet and laid them in her palm.

'I'll see you in the john,' she said, taking her worn canvas bag from the seat next to her.

After a few minutes Jim made his way there.

She was standing at the back, past the urinals, outside the only clean cubicle. The place stank of urine. Patty stared at the piss on the floor as Jim walked in and put a broom against the door.

'Well, hallelujah baby,' he said, rubbing his hands together.

'Come on,' she said, walking into the cubicle, pulling down her jeans.

'You're as sweet as cherry pie, ain't you?'

'Put this on,' she said, pulling a condom out of her faded denim jacket.

'That's like playing the piano with gloves on.'

'Well, Beethoven, it's either that or no pussy.'

'You really want me to put that thing on?'

She crossed her arms and waited for him to do it.

'Give me a little help here,' Jim said, unzipping his fly.

She touched him and thought of food, a bed for the night as Jim tore the packet open with his teeth and pulled the condom out.

'Happy now?' he said.

She leaned back against the wall and saw endless miles of road as his skin made contact. He shoved his right hand inside her blouse and groped her breasts. His skin was callused and felt like sandpaper on her nipples. She thought she heard someone trying the door as he entered her.

'You're safe with me, but you sure picked a bad place to stop,' he said. 'If I was you I'd get out of here, this place will eat you alive.'

She looked over Jim's shoulder at a fly crawling across the graffiti. Someone had scrawled 'Animals' on the chipped and tarnished paint. She looked into his eyes and watched them empty of desire. She felt the cold wall against her buttocks as he stopped.

He winked and ran his finger across her cheek.

'Told you I ain't the maniac trucker.'

After he left she heard a pickup drive off as she readjusted her clothes and checked herself in the mirror.

Then the door swung open and the waitress walked in.

'I knew it,' she said. 'I saw him leave, I'm calling the po-lice.'

'Why you such a bitch?'

'You just made a big mistake, you hooker.'

'You don't get to call me no hooker. You're just a fucking waitress.'

'You don't belong here.'

'Belong where? This is nowhere.'

'We have regular customers who like things a certain way. You don't muscle in on territory that ain't yours. I'm giving you two minutes to git.'

The diner was filling up when Patty went back outside. The waitress was smiling at a trucker in faded Wranglers and blue suede cowboy boots who was leaning on the counter.

'What can I get you Pete?' the waitress said to him.

'Oh, just a coffee.'

Patty headed outside and stood among the women who were gathering to trade sex. They wore hot pants and halter tops, some of them sheer blouses. She looked at her clothes. Her blouse was missing a button, and her bra showed through the gap.

'Hey, how about it?' a large man with a thick matted beard said.

'I don't think so.'

Patty wandered off as she heard the women talk among themselves.

A black Chevrolet drove past her and pulled into the truck stop. A tall lean man in a red coat got out and walked over to the women. He stood there with his hands in his pockets, said something to a small dark prostitute in a black skirt, nodded, and then entered the diner. He waved at the waitress.

'Evenin' Theodore,' she said. 'We have some fresh pizza.'

'Sounds good, I'll just use your restroom.'

The waitress continued chatting to Pete. She didn't pay any attention to the prostitute in the black skirt who wandered in, the waitress merely glanced at her, then touched up her lipstick using a makeup mirror that she pulled from her purse. The woman went to join Theodore in the cubicle Patty had recently vacated. She was in her early twenties but had the used look of a life that held no pleasure except the diminishing high she got each night as she shot up.

Theodore didn't look at her but waited as she pulled up her skirt, slipped down her G-string, and fumbled with his fly. He lifted her halter top. His small black eyes gazed at her breasts. She leaned against the door and Theodore entered her. She didn't look at his face as he penetrated her. Theodore began to sweat as he increased his rhythm, and the smell of grease broke from his pores. When he stopped he ran his hand through his thick black hair and stared up at the ceiling, then pulled out and zipped up. He counted out the cash and waited until she left.

He was washing his hands at the cracked sink thinking about the meat loaf the diner served when the door opened. Then someone reached over his shoulder and ran a straight razor across his neck. Theodore never got to see his killer. He was holding his hands to the wound as the door closed. He staggered across the room and collapsed by the urinals. As he lay there drowning in his own blood, it looked like his red coat was melting into the urine.

2.

1:00 a.m.

Patty didn't see the ambulance arrive at the diner. She'd caught a ride from a driver who smelt of beer and onions.

'I figured you were looking to trade,' he said after they'd travelled in silence for a few miles.

'Trade what?'

'What do you think?'

'I'm just trying to get somewhere.'

'We're all trying to get somewhere.'

He winked at her and put a CD into the dashboard player, yanking the volume up and pulling a can of Coors from a cooler that sat by Patty's legs. His hand brushed her thigh as Aerosmith's 'Flesh' started to pound the inside of the cab. He tilted his head back and swigged from the can. Patty glanced at him, taking in his thick neck and broad shoulders. His heavy hands rested on the wheel as if it was a toy. He turned and stared at her with cold green eyes that looked like marbles in his suntanned skin.

'Look, I just need a ride,' she said.

'Where to? All you told me when you climbed in is you're heading the way I'm going.'

'Next town along here.'

'You're going nowhere, ain't you sweetheart?'

'Excuse me, but I ain't your sweetheart.'

'And whose might you be?'

Patty leaned forward and turned the music off.

'Hey, I thought we were going to have a party,' the driver said.

'I hate parties.'

'Aw come on, we got the night.'

'Can you let me out?'

'You only just got in.'

'I know.'

'Look, I was just messing with you. Forgive me. It gets boring on the road all day, and sometimes I lose perspective. My name's Red.'

He reached out his hand, and Patty took it briefly and sat back against the door.

She stared out at the black highway. There were no cars, no trucks, no houses visible.

'I didn't catch your name,' Red said.

'Call me Patty.'

'Well, Patty, there's cold beer if you want one.'

She opened a can and sipped from it. She could see some sandwiches in a torn plastic bag next to the box.

'Hungry?' Red said.

'Not really.'

'When was the last time you ate?'

'I had something at the diner.'

'Strange place.'

'You could say that.'

'Come on Patty, have a bite,' Red said, picking up a sandwich, opening it, and offering half to her. 'Cheese, won't hurt you any. And besides, next town's a ways.'

'I thought it was a few miles.'

'Now I don't know where you think you are, but there's nothing out here. I mean nothing, just a few snakes and me.'

Patty took the sandwich from him. The bread felt hard and stale.

'So deserted. What is it with Arizona?'

'Arizona? You ain't in Arizona.'

'Well where am I?'

'You're in a wilderness run by animals, sweetheart.'

'I told you not to call me that.'

'OK, OK,' he said, turning towards her, holding both hands up before him. You sound like my ex.'

'Would you keep your hands on the wheel?'

'There's nowhere else I can put them unless I play with myself.'

'What's the next town called?'

'Nothing, really. It's just a place where a few people live out their bitter lives.'

She looked at the landscape. She saw shapes move and blur like deformed nocturnal sculptures.

'Why bitter?'

'Most people you're going to meet here are ruined in some way, they need to be.'

'You're messing with me again.'

'I'm not. I tell you this is one weird place.'

'You're not from around here.'

He nodded.

'Massachusetts. I got into trucking to escape.'

'Escape from what?'

'You really want to know?'

'Since you bring it up.'

'Something I saw.'

'You mean a crime?'

'You could call it that, although I'm not on the run. What I saw wasn't some shooting by a gang or Mafia heist or a robbery. I'm not afraid someone's gonna come and get me, pop me, 'cause I'm a witness. No, what I saw etched itself into my mind, and the only way I can remove it is to use the constant backdrop of the highway.'

'Etched? You have a fancy way with words for a trucker.'

'I like words. I like women more. I ain't your average trucker.'

'So what was it? This thing you saw that messed you up.'

'I'm a big fella, as you can see. I used to be a psychiatric nurse. I could hold down the crazies, and I tell you they got the strength of a tiger when it's in them. I seen that thing enter the minds of men who were half my size, and they could throw a man like me across the room.'

'What thing?'

'I don't know what to call it. It's like some light or an absence of light, and I'll never figure out which, but they become absorbed by something, an entity if you will. Light and darkness are strange phenomena. I look out the window of my cab so often at night and see a light hover on the landscape, and in some of the brightest lit places I go to, the people seem empty. Maybe this won't make any sense to you, but I saw something. The light I'm talking about doesn't come from the sun, but somewhere else.'

'What did you see when you were a nurse?'

'The man I'm talking about wasn't normal by any standards, none of the people in that place were, but he was extreme. You don't want to look into his eyes. One day he assaulted a nurse, broke the guy's jaw like he was popping a bubble. Then he abducted a female nurse. I found him in his room, straddling her. She'd lost her shoes in the scuffle, and she was kicking out beneath him. All I could see was his back and her legs. Then I walked around and saw what he was doing to her.'

'What was he doing to her?'

'He was eating her face.'

'Jesus.'

'It took four of us to pull him off her. Her jawbone was showing through the ragged flesh. It's an image that I'll never forget, no matter how many miles I drive, or how much beer I drink. He stood there with her skin all over his mouth, like he was wearing the mask of a ghoul. He looked straight at me and said, "I feed off the road. I live on the savage highway." Then he spat a piece of the nurse's chin at me.'

'What did they do to him?'

'Drugged him. He was so far beyond the criminal that he made no sense in terms of the law. He was going to stay there for life. He'd been sent there for setting fire to a cop. But afterwards, a few days before I left the job, we found out the other things he'd done.'

'And what were they?'

'He'd been collecting heads. I'm told the cellar of his house was packed floor to ceiling with the bleached skulls of unknown men and women.'

'Is this for real?'

'Unfortunately, yes.'

'Pretty creepy stuff.'

'Creepy? No. Creepy is a guy feeling your thigh at a bus stop. This goes far beyond creepy.'

'Well, he'll never get out.'

Red stared out at the highway. Patty noticed he'd slowed his speed.

'Some months later, after I left, they moved him to a new facility for the criminally insane. He escaped in transit.'

'How?'

'We'll never know, but the two guards were both found decapitated.'

'He's still on the loose.'

'The police all over Massachusetts looked for him, but he was never found.'

'How long ago was this?'

'A few years.'

'Sooner or later the law will catch up with him. What was his name?'

Red pulled a pack of Marlboros from his pocket and lit a cigarette.

'Donald Lake.'

In the light of the Zippo his face looked as though it was burning, and Patty noticed a long scar on his cheek and neck that faded at the collar of his chequered lumberjack shirt. His hand bore the tattoo of a woman in chains and some kind of animal.

'What's the tattoo?' Patty said.

'What's it look like to you?'

'A chick. What's the animal?'

'The animal is whatever you want it to be.'

'Is it a wolf?'

'Looks like a wolf, don't it?'

On closer inspection the animal appeared to have a man's body.

'How much further to the town?' Patty said.

'Why are you in a hurry?'

'I want to get some sleep.'

'You can sleep right here.'

'I never can, moving.'

'Do you think I'm going to touch you? That ain't my way. I like them live and kicking.'

'Kicking?'

'Just an expression.'

'You want some tail, all you need to do is turn this truck around and head back to the diner.'

'You mean the hookers? Now they're a sight for sore eyes.'

'You approve of exploitation?'

'Exploitation? I think it's the other way around, the money they charge. Have you seen some of them?'

'They're addicted.'

'Addicted to selling their pussies. You never sold it for a little cash?'

'Those women have no choice.'

'How do you know?'

'I just do.'

'You sure are talkative all of a sudden when sex is

mentioned. Maybe I ought to take you out back and slide it inside you and see how you squeal out here in the dark.'

'That ain't funny.'

'Patty how about shedding them clothes and showing me your hot little thing?'

'Is that how I pay for the ride?'

'A lot of women like it rough and hard. That's what my wife never understood.'

'What?'

'I only did it the one time, to show her how much pleasure a girl can get. Held her down with a pillow over her face while I lifted up her skirt.'

'Let me out.'

'You picked the wrong truck darling.' He looked at her, dropping his eyes to the hint of bra that showed through the missing button. 'I've screwed all the hookers at that diner. I ain't never seen you, and I want a little action. Is that so hard to understand?'

'No.'

'I'll pull over, and we can go in the back of the truck. I got a bed back there, real nice, subdued lighting. You're lucky you picked Red. You probably heard the stories about women getting into trucks and never being seen again. I know a few truckers who are into that kind of thing. They fuck 'em and beat 'em up. All I want is to stick it in your snatch.'

'That's all?'

He pulled the truck over at the side of the highway.

'That's all.'

Patty picked up her bag and climbed out. She could see some lights in the distance.

'I need to pee,' she said.

'Don't be shy,' Red said, walking around to her side of the truck.

Patty walked a few feet to a bank that ran down to some bushes. She began to clamber down.

'Not too far, do it there,' Red said.

He stepped towards her. She turned her back, lowered her jeans, and squatted. She figured it would take him a few seconds to reach her. When she finished, she pulled her jeans back up, grabbed her bag, and dived down the bank, cutting herself on brambles. She could hear Red coming after her, branches breaking beneath his weight, and she went straight into the bushes, tangling her clothes, tearing her skin, running until she emerged on the other side in a field beneath a pale moon. Then she stopped and listened to the silence. In the distance was a small town, and Patty walked towards it as dawn began to leak pink light into the trees.

Red was a few miles away as she approached the town. He was talking into his cell phone.

'She went through the field, she's heading your way,' he said.

His truck cut through the dawn like a juggernaut as he set his cold eyes on the highway.

3.

Johnny Sullivan pulled his Jeep into the small town of Purity. He got out, stretched, and looked around at the neat row of shops and the white houses bearing American flags, feeling as though he'd stepped straight into a picture postcard of an ideal America. The landscape looked hilly in the distance, a green and undulating enclave as incongruous as an oasis. He was a tall man with a lean, well-muscled physique. He had pale blue eyes and a boxer's nose. He wandered down Main Street in search of somewhere to eat. There was no one about, and the pristine front windows of the houses looked like mirrors, reflective and as unyielding as camera lenses. The town reminded Johnny of a film set, and the street held the unreality of a neatly constructed facade which hid something ruinous.

That morning there was not a single car parked on the gentle drives that led in easy gradients from road to home. There were no leaves on the immaculate manicured lawns that looked both unnatural and abandoned. But what fascinated Johnny the most was the absence of litter. There was no breeze, and the air seemed static beneath a blinding sun.

The anomaly of Porter's Café lay at the end of the wide

deserted street, exuding the smell of freshly baked bread and home cooking. A woman with bobbed brown hair was standing at the open door as he approached. She went behind the counter and began to wipe a large plate, looking at Johnny with quiet curiosity as he walked in.

'I was hoping I could get some breakfast,' he said.

'I can do you some bacon, bread, waffles, grits,' she said.

'Do you have any fresh coffee while I wait?'

'I'll bring one over.'

Johnny stood there for a few moments looking at her. She was an attractive woman, in her mid-thirties he guessed. She wore a white uniform that had a yellow stain on the bosom. It fitted her full, voluptuous figure snugly.

Johnny went and sat by the window. The owner seemed intrigued by him, taking in every detail of his dress as she made his breakfast, moving between kitchen and counter, a silent and watchful presence. Johnny wore some Levis and trainers that held dried mud on their soles. He had one foot up against the chair, his leg bouncing up and down. He had a dark blue windbreaker on and beneath it a dull washed out T-shirt.

As she set his coffee down on the table she met his clear blue eyes with a steady gaze.

'Now that smells good,' he said.

'Passing through?'

'I'm not entirely sure.'

'We don't get many strangers here.'

'Am I that strange?'

'That's not what I meant.'

'I was just trying to engage you in conversation, the habit of a lonely man.'

'I know about loneliness. Purity is pretty cut off.'

She went into the kitchen. Johnny felt drowsy and began to nod off. The frying oil sounded like rain falling outside and he began to dream of his house in Ontario set amid fields that acted as a blanket to the outside world.

He felt disoriented as she woke him by setting his plate down. He stared up into her dark eyes, momentarily unaware of where he was.

'I've been driving all night,' he said.

'The coffee ought to wake you up.'

'Join me,' he said, pulling out the chair opposite him.

She hesitated.

'If I get customers I'll have to go back.'

'Johnny Sullivan,' he said, extending his hand.

Her palm felt warm and soft in his.

'Natasha Porter,' she said, sitting down.

'As on the door.'

She nodded.

He cut into the bacon and put a piece in his mouth.

'This is really good,' he said.

'So what brings you here, Johnny?'

'A few weeks ago, my life changed.'

'Oh?'

'I lost my job. Then my wife walked out on me.'

'I'm sorry to hear that.'

He looked at her, noticing her full, erotic mouth as she touched the tip of her tongue to her lips.

'I decided to take to the road in search of a story.'

'A story?'

'I was a sports journalist, quite a good one, I'm told. I covered many big games, and the reason I lost my job is because I was dumb.'

'You don't strike me as stupid.'

'Do you think exposing corruption is worthwhile?'

'That's a hard question to answer. Mind if I smoke?'

'Not at all. Hasn't the ban reached Arizona?'

Natasha frowned and tapped a Chesterfield loose from its pack.

'I don't care about any ban, this is my place.'

'Well said.'

'Besides, this area does as it pleases.'

She tore a match loose from a bright blue book that displayed the silhouette of a woman in a cocktail dress and the name 'Sloppy Joe's' in shiny gold letters. She struck it and held the flaming match to the cigarette, took a deep drag, pursed her lips, then blew a plume of smoke towards the door.

'So, what's with you and corruption, Johnny?'

'I uncovered something, bribes passing backwards and forwards, match-fixing. I believe that sort of thing ruins sport, everyone suffers, the game, the fans most of all. I exposed it, wrote an article. And then I was called into the editor's office one rainy Monday morning. An hour later I was clearing my desk.'

'Yeah, doing the right thing gets you punished, especially in a world where crime is rewarded.'

'I started as an investigative reporter. I was trained to uncover lies. You try telling a bloodhound not to follow the scent of deer.'

'So what happened to your wife?'

'I'd been working long hours. We'd hardly spoken for years. We'd meet at weekends and do the things married couples do, those empty acts that take a little of the time you don't want to spend with the person you're meant to be spending it with. I told her I'd been fired. She went shopping. She came back with bags of dresses, paid for with my credit card. Then she sat down in front of me, about the same distance as you're sitting from me. She said, "Johnny, I'm having an affair. I've been having an affair for two years now, and I'm leaving you." The next day she was gone. She packed all her things and left. I spent two weeks drinking hard. Then I headed out onto the open road.'

'Do you miss her?'

'Not really.'

'I can understand that, empty marriages and all.'

'And you, Natasha, are you married?'

'Unfortunately.'

'It's like that, is it?'

'Worse.'

'Why don't you leave him?'

'Some men won't be left.'

'You don't look like a prisoner to me.'

'Purity belongs in an Edward Hopper painting, Johnny. Sometimes I feel I'm in one of his depictions of the vacuum at the heart of America.'

'So what keeps you here?'

'Fear, guilt, disease, hatred, I don't know. Look around at the town that's a living lie, purity doesn't exist here.'

'Sounds like I stumbled into the right place.'

'Yeah? Well stumble right out again, get onto the highway and drive away, keep driving because you don't want to stay here.'

'Is there anywhere to stay?'

She stubbed out her cigarette in a plastic ashtray on the end of the table.

'We got a four-room hotel with faded wallpaper bearing nail marks, not from a moment of passion, no, those marks you'll see are from all the people who know despair like a constant toothache. Go to sleep on the soiled sheets of Purity's only hotel, spend a few nights here, and you'll begin to scream with claustrophobia. And you can laugh your heart out at its name. Welcome to the Morality Inn.'

'You'll never make it as a tourist adviser.'

'I'm not joking. Where is it you come from Johnny?'

'Ontario, New York.'

'Go back.'

'All that you've said has left me wondering.'

'Wondering what?'

'About this place.'

'It'll make you wonder all right. So what's the story you're searching for, Johnny?'

He took a sip from his coffee and placed the mug on the table.

'A lot of women have gone missing in this part of Arizona.'

'Lucky them.'

'I don't think so.'

'What do you think happened to them beyond running off with some man who might be a bit more stimulating than their creep husbands?'

'That's what I want to find out.'

'Yeah, well, I'll tell you you're wasting your time.'

'Have you noticed what happens at the truck stops?'

'You mean a bunch of fat bearded men eat huge amounts of cholesterol? That seems pretty standard.'

'No, I'm not talking about that.'

'Then what are you talking about?'

'The prostitution. It's quite apparent. You can see the women coming out after dark, the dollars changing hands.'

'Nothing's apparent, Johnny, nothing at all.'

'I think they're being abducted.'

'By who?'

'That's what I intend to find out.'

'It's a pretty town, ain't it? But everything around here's different in the dark.'

Natasha stood up and went behind the counter. Johnny finished eating, then went over to the till and paid.

'I didn't mean to ask too many questions,' he said.

'It don't bother me. You just brought back a memory, that's all.'

She handed him his change.

'No, keep it, thank you for the company.'

'I'd just keep driving if I was you, there's nothing here except heartache.'

Johnny turned and left. He walked back to his Jeep. As he started the engine he saw a police car draw up outside the cafe and two officers get out. He watched them walk inside, then he drove on to the end of Main Street where the Morality Inn stood next to a small green. He stopped and got out and walked into the musty reception area. A brass bell stood on a gnarled desk on which some faded flowers gave off a dank aroma. He looked around, taking in the threadbare red carpet and the pictures of men holding fish on the walls. Then he rang the bell.

As Johnny checked in, officers Harry Reed and Mitch Samuels were talking to Natasha.

Reed was a heavyset man who ate too much pasta, worked out with weights, and had been told by his doctor to lose twelve pounds. Samuels was wiry and walked with a slow strut.

They took their hats off as they went into the café.

'Mrs. Mills?' Reed said.

'I prefer to use my maiden name, Porter, now what can I get you gentleman?'

Reed looked at Samuels and back at Natasha.

'Your husband is Theodore Mills?' he said.

Natasha put her finger to her chin.

'Now let me think, yes, that name is unfortunately familiar.'

'Ma'am, you'll have to come with us.'

'Why, what have I done?'

'You haven't done anything. I'm sorry to inform you that your husband's been killed.'

'Killed? By which of the many people who hate his guts?'

Reed paused and looked down at his hat, the brim balanced between his hands.

'We need you to identify the body,' Samuels said.

'I guess there's no one else,' she said.

She went into the kitchen and removed her uniform. Then she went outside, locked the café, and got into the police car with them.

4.

That evening a man in a black shirt entered Purity. He had black hair and eyes that hovered between turquoise and green, and he moved with the ease of an athlete. He walked halfway down Main Street and rang the bell on a house. After a few moments Natasha opened the door.

'Valentino, I'm so glad you're here,' she said.

'There's only one reason I come to Purity.'

She stepped aside and let him in. She didn't bother closing the door as she took his face in her hands and kissed him, putting her tongue deep into his mouth and pressing her body against his. She looked into his eyes, placed her palm against his cheek, and touched his chest.

'He's gone,' she said.

'The husband?'

'Someone's killed him. We've no need to hide.'

'Who do you think did it?'

Natasha shrugged. Then she closed the door, unbuttoned her blouse, and took Valentino by the hand as she walked towards the bedroom.

Upstairs she undid Valentino's shirt and slipped out of

her skirt. He caressed her gently in the darkened room.

'Only you know how to touch me,' she said.

There was hunger and sadness in her as she took from this man the things she'd always craved. She got on top of him on the bed and took him inside her, her ankles tight against his legs. And as she found her pleasure she pushed away the fear that lay beneath the fulfilment his body offered hers. Afterwards, she lay next to him and ran her finger along the pale white scar on his right shoulder.

'I used to dream about a man like you. I was lost in this small town with only my bitterness to keep me company.'

'It's understandable you're bitter, after all he put you through.'

'You never told me where you got this.'

He looked at her finger on his dark skin.

'That? Some men I knew wanted something from me I didn't have.'

'They cut you.'

'They wanted money. It happens a lot in my country. Many of my friends are dead. I couldn't pay them, so one of them stabbed me as a warning. They gave me a few days to get the cash, and they came back.'

'What happened?'

'I killed them. I put two bullets in each of their heads. They wanted to rape my sister because I couldn't pay them, and I couldn't allow that.'

'I've heard about the rape houses in Mexico.'

'There are many vanished women.'

'I feel like I've been living in a rape house myself, but he's gone.'

'Your husband was a sexual sadist. Rape in all its forms

is an addiction to a man like him.'

'He's left his mark inside me. But you take away the scars.'

'And what now that he's gone?'

She sat up and looked down at him. His eyes always seemed focused and gave nothing away, and she hungered for this man about whom she knew so little and from whom she wanted everything. Valentino reached up and touched her breasts.

'No more hiding. No more cheap hotels and motels on the edge of nowhere,' she said. 'No more hurried good-byes. No more nights when I have to stop myself from calling you and begging you to come and get me and take me away from Purity. No more missing you.'

'And here I am on my white charger.'

'Honey, don't you see? He's gone. That animal got his dues, and we're free to do what we want.'

'Is anyone free?'

'Maybe the ruined are.'

'He didn't ruin you, Natasha.'

'You know, the first time he did it I was packing to leave. He threatened me with worse. I knew I'd have nothing and him and his friends would track me to whatever state I went to and do things he described that I still can't shake out of my head. He showed me pictures of some of the women. What he was into was really dark. I mean, if Theodore didn't inflict fear and pain there was no turn-on to him. He tried hiding it from me when we were first married, but it came out. It was the strongest part of him.'

'He was a torturer of the purest kind.'

'I could tell the cops were looking at me waiting for the

grief, but there is none.'

'Where was he killed?'

'At the diner he owned a part stake in. He was probably screwing a hooker there. Someone came up behind him in the john and sliced his throat back.'

'Who do you think it was?'

'Who knows?'

'Natasha, your bad times are over.'

'Help me find my way into my body again. The things he did to me have locked me out of myself.'

She took him inside her and found release from the memories that so often deprived her of sleep. That night the dreams that came to her were not of Theodore raping her on the kitchen floor beneath the bouquets of bloodred roses whose perfume haunted her and whose colour she detested, nor of the things that she discovered about him and Purity itself, but of a time when long ago she felt young and intact.

When she awoke the next morning, Valentino was in the bathroom shaving. She got up and looked out of the bedroom window. The sun was beating down on the grass, and the street was swathed in light. Natasha went into the bathroom and watched Valentino flick suds into the sink and looked at his hard muscles ripple beneath his tanned skin. She went downstairs and made some coffee. She was standing in the kitchen in a T-shirt that stopped at the tops of her thighs when the doorbell rang. She opened it part way and peered out into the bright street.

'I thought I ought to tell you.'

'Tell me what, Morgan?' she said.

'About your old man.'

'I already know.'

Morgan Lane was six foot eight, heavily built, and covered in tattoos. Natasha could see oil in his thick unkempt beard, and his truck parked outside her house.

'Ain't you gonna invite me in? For old times' sake?'

'There aren't any old times. You and me were over long before it happened, and frankly I wish it hadn't.'

'It ain't like you to be shy. And besides, you know I can see your poontang through that skinny little thing. You offering me breakfast?'

'Get out.'

She tried to close the door, but he had his hand on it and pushed his way into the hall as Valentino came downstairs in a pair of black Levis and a gleaming white western-style shirt.

'Oh, so you got yourself a fancy man?' Morgan said. 'Enjoy her, Romeo, most of the town has.'

'You don't talk to a lady like that,' Valentino said.

'Lady? What truck did you get off?'

'I didn't get off a truck.'

'Morgan was just leaving,' Natasha said.

'Was I?' He ran his eyes down her body, then glanced at Valentino. 'You think this guy's going to stick around you?'

'Get out, Morgan.'

'I'm going. You ain't worth more than the two-dollar whores up the road, and he'll find that out. I only came by to tell you your old man got cut to death. But I guess that don't matter seeing how you're already hitched up with some other guy, which I'm sure the cops will be interested to find out. How much money did Theodore leave you?'

'I think it's time you turned around,' Valentino said.

'Are you threatening me, boy?'

'I'm not a boy, are you?'

Morgan stepped towards him.

'I'm all sorts of things, and I'm certainly not what you'd want to meet on the dark highway.'

'I imagine that not many people want to meet you at all.'

'Is that so? Something's not right here. A male whore, that's all you are. Why would you want to stick it in a used up piece of snatch like hers?'

'I think you've said enough,' Valentino said.

'I rode her for a while, I know what she's like.'

'You certainly know how to cheapen yourself,' Valentino said.

'Maybe you killed Theodore and you're after her money. What's your name?'

'Valentino.'

'Valentino? Now that's a hoot. Natasha if you'd told me you like male buffalo I'd have got you some, and me and the boys could've watched you get it on.'

'You're a voyeur, is that it?' Valentino said.

'You better not run into me again,' Morgan said and left.

Natasha closed the door and went into the kitchen. She could hear his truck start up outside as she poured some coffee.

'I'm sorry about that,' she said.

'He's certainly a study in frustration.'

'He didn't bother you?'

'Why would he bother me?'

'Morgan can get kind of rough.'

'Was he like that with you?'

'No. I slept with him a few times, and I regret it. The

only reason I did was because he offered to help me with Theodore, said he knew all about what he was into. I know it wasn't right. I'm not attracted to a man like that. Then I found out he and Theodore were buddies, and he threatened to tell him. He blackmailed me, and he frightens me. He has a violent reputation with the truckers. He likes hurting people, and he hurts them real bad.'

'Forget about him.'

'I think I'll take a shower. He's kind of needled me.'

'A man like that?'

'Honey, you could have your pick of any woman. Why are you with me?'

'Don't let him get to you,' Valentino said.

5.

When Morgan left Purity he drove to a truck stop on the edge of the next town. He got out and walked over to a food stand and ordered a burger and a Coke, squirting ketchup all over the greasy meat. As he took his first bite, another truck pulled up and the driver got out.

'Hey, Red,' Morgan said.

'How you doing, buddy?' Red said.

'Not too bad, apart from a little aggravation from some old pussy.'

'You ought to get yourself some highway action, Bubba.'

'Maybe you and I should cruise for some one night.'

'Tired of commercial company?'

'Tired of here, is all. So how about it, we could do a two-man job on some roadside snatch.'

'Ah, I prefer working on my own.'

'And why is that?' Morgan said, biting into the burger, the ketchup smearing across his lips.

'Just like to focus on the job.'

'You just like 'em all to yourself. Any news on the missing girl?'

'The one the other night? No, she only had one place to go.'

'I looked in Purity after you called me, but I didn't see her. Where do you think she is?'

'Who knows? If I catch up with her again I'll make sure we get her to the destination.'

'Yeah, there's only one place for a lot lizard like her to go.'

'We gotta keep the pickle parks tight.'

'I better get on,' Morgan said.

Red watched him walk away, then ordered a Pepsi and some fries and sat in his truck eating them, staring out at a slate grey sky that was empty of birds, his eyes as diaphanous as cut glass. Then he turned on his engine and got back on the highway.

The truck stop was within walking distance of the town that sat below some hills. Scarsdale housed about a hundred people. Red might have been interested to know that at that moment it also housed Patty. She was dressing in the small hotel room she'd stayed in since she ran away from him.

Patty had been about half a mile from Purity when she changed direction. She thought about what she'd do if she was Red, and she figured she'd drive straight to the only town visible. She guessed he was waiting for her there, so she kept on walking until she found Scarsdale. Then she booked into the Hungry Traveller and slept for hours.

That morning she got up late, had breakfast in her room, and left the hotel at about 1:00 p.m. and walked to the local bar. It began to rain as she sat in The Bounty, and Patty stared at the drops hitting the ground and forming puddles. She ordered two fingers of Jack Daniels neat and sipped it, feeling the warmth spread across her belly as she wondered how much longer the money she'd taken from Jim would last. Outside a Jeep pulled up, and Johnny got out. He held a magazine over his head as he ran towards the bar, his trainers splashing in the puddles.

Patty ordered a club sandwich from the bartender as Johnny entered, shaking the raindrops from his coat. He came up and sat on the next stool.

'What can I get you?' the bartender said.

'I'll have a Bud, maybe something to eat.'

'Specials are on the board, or we got sandwiches.'

The bartender, a large man with a potbelly, slid the menu towards Johnny. Patty watched him in the polished mirror behind the bar. Johnny looked up, and there was a moment when their gazes held then broke.

'I'll have the ham on wheat,' Johnny said.

He opened the magazine, a copy of *AZ Sports and Lifestyle* and sat there reading it as the bartender slid his beer across the bar.

'You're not from around here?' the bartender said.

Johnny put the magazine down and looked up.

'No, I guess I'm passing through.'

'Well there ain't much to see.'

'I've found many sleepy American towns to be quite interesting.'

'Is that right?'

'I'm sure in your line of work you see some unusual things. I know in my job I do.'

'And what is it you do?'

'I'm a journalist.'

'What kind of journalist?'

'Sports.'

'Now that must be one great job.'

'It is, when you're not dealing with scams.'

'My name's Al, by the way.'

He reached his hand across the bar.

'Johnny.'

Al went through to the kitchen and came back with Patty's sandwich.

'Staying locally?' he said to her.

'I'll probably hitch a ride out of here.'

'Not exciting enough for you?'

'I wouldn't say I'm looking for excitement.'

'I can't place your accent,' Al said.

'I was born in New York.'

Johnny reached out his hand.

'I'm from Ontario,' he said.

Patty hesitated, then shook it.

'I'm Patty.'

'Pleased to meet you.'

'You working on a story out here?' Al said.

'I am.'

'Baseball?'

'The story I'm working on has nothing to do with sport.'

'So, it's like a travel piece?'

'More a local story. Perhaps you can help me.'

'If I know anything,' Al said.

Johnny sipped his beer and wiped the froth from his mouth.

'Have you known anyone to disappear from this area?'

'No.'

'A number of women have gone missing on the highway.'

'I don't know nothing about that.'

'A lot of young women, some of them prostitutes, have hitched rides and never been seen again.'

'That's a new one on me,' Al said.

'What's your theory?' Patty said.

'I think there may be a killer operating in the area.'

Al folded his arms.

'Heck, Scarsdale's one of the safest towns in America.'

He went out back and brought Johnny his sandwich. Then he walked into the small office between the bar and the reception area and made a call.

'I heard you say you're hitching,' Johnny said to Patty.

'That's right.'

'I don't mean to alarm you, but it's not the safest place to do that.'

'I know.'

'Have you heard about the missing women?'

'I haven't, but I nearly was one.'

'Oh?'

'A few nights ago I hitched a ride from a guy called Red. He started off with this crazy talk, I thought he was messing with me, then he threatened to rape me and talked about some madman he knew who ate a woman's face. The whole thing got real scary. I got out of the truck in the middle of nowhere and ran.'

'You're lucky you got away.'

'I'd say.'

'Would you give me a description of this man?'

Patty finished her whisky.

'Large guy, heavily built, strong, thick neck. Oh, and he had a scar, here.' She traced the mark across her own face. 'How do you plan to find out what's going on?'

'I'm trying to figure out where the women are being taken to. I think I know where they're being abducted from.'

'Where?'

'Truck stops.'

'I've seen the hookers at work. I think he mistook me for one.'

'You really shouldn't hitch any more rides.'

'So what are you gonna do?'

'I want to find out if there's been an investigation into the disappearances.'

'Have you spoken to the cops?'

'Not yet. I want to be able to hand them something solid, and from what I know there have been no arrests at all. Whoever's doing this is picking vagrants, hookers, people no one cares about. If you went missing, Patty, would anyone come looking for you?'

'Are you asking me if I have family?'

'I'm saying do you have anyone?'

'Everyone has someone, Johnny.'

'Not everyone.'

'How did you find all this out?'

'A colleague of mine was working on the story. He told me he was convinced he was on the verge of a big scoop. He said he knew for certain at least one hundred women had gone missing. He also told me he'd come up against police corruption.'

'You said he was working on the story, what happened?'

'He vanished a few months ago.'

She watched Johnny take a bite of his sandwich.

'Have you heard of the maniac trucker?' Patty said.

'I don't believe I have.'

'Well I can tell you what some creep told me before I hitched my ride with Red. I was having a smoke at a stop, and this guy got talking to me. He said a man is out there on the highway chopping women up. He called him the maniac trucker and added he heard this guy drove a pickup.'

'Did you get his name?'

'He called himself Jim.'

Johnny took a pen from his pocket and scribbled on the back of the magazine.

'You don't mind?' he said.

'Go ahead.'

'It would make sense that this man is a trucker.'

'So who do you think this is, a lone predator who rapes and kills his victims?'

'I think he tortures them.'

6.

Director Sam Roche spent several minutes humiliating officers Harry Reed and Mitch Samuels after they returned from dropping Natasha back at the café. Roche stood at six two and had muscles as hard as timber. His biceps looked as though they were about to tear his shirt as he flexed his arms during his dressing-down of his men.

'Why the fuck didn't you ask her questions? The woman is known to have hated Theodore, a respected local businessman who put money into this force. She sees other men, you catch my drift? The woman ain't no better than a goddamned whore, offering it up to any passing stranger, and now I hear from a good source she's moved her fancy man in. So a man is killed and his wife carries on like that, who's the suspect? It ain't the president. You boys are worse than pussies. I'm gonna have a word with her. I might have to field you out to Yuma. And Reed, lose some fucking weight.'

Reed and Samuels went outside as Roche picked up the phone.

'Morgan, this guy you told me about, the one who calls himself Valentino, I want you to keep an eye on him and that lying whore. I want to pull his jacket, heck he's a spic. He belongs behind bars, not inside Theodore's wife.'

Roche slammed the phone down and stood there with his fists clenched. His knuckles looked as sharp as rocks. The wall displayed various pictures of him smiling, and from a distance his face and demeanour seemed benevolent, but his teeth were too sharp and the smile was forced. He had neatly cut silver hair and cold, dead eyes.

Sam Roche had become district director of the Yuma department of the Arizona Highway Patrol at the age of 42. He always said he protected the highways from the wrong types.

Roche delegated many of his duties at Yuma when he started running a new station in that indeterminate area between Purity and Friskford, which covered the section of highway in which he was particularly interested. It was a relatively unpopulated area that he felt needed his individual style of policing.

The building he worked in was funded by local businessmen, among them Theodore Mills. The station was new, and Roche hadn't disclosed its existence to the higher authorities of the Arizona Highway Patrol. It had a first-rate canteen and its own arsenal, and Roche and his assistant, Deputy Director Franklin Norman, had bulletproof windows in their offices. Roche and Norman visited the Yuma department intermittently, maintaining their positions there. The original officers who worked there remained there while Roche recruited new officers for his new station.

He had a large house just outside Scarsdale, which he shared with his wife, Sandra. Their two kids had moved out years ago, feeling they'd failed their father. Roche had never openly criticised them, but it was clear from the way he treated them that he viewed them as a duty he had to perform. He'd never wanted children but had given them to Sandra in the early days of their marriage when she complained of loneliness. Roche worked hard, and Sandra bore their marriage as if it was an alternative to something worse. He didn't treat her badly. He never drank, since his father had died of alcoholism, but he held the alcoholic's rage inside him and had other vices he kept away from his home. But Sandra felt alone and conscious of the distance between her and her husband.

That afternoon Roche got in his police car and drove to Purity.

Natasha was in the empty café when she saw him get out of his car and walk up. He closed the door, bolted it, and displayed the closed sign.

'What do you think you're doing?' Natasha said.

'I'll have a coffee, make it fresh, then you and I are going to have a little chat.'

He walked behind the counter as she poured it. Natasha handed the mug to him and took a few steps back.

'In there,' he said, motioning to the kitchen with his head.

'What's wrong with out here where we can be seen?'

'What I've got to say won't take long, and it's of a private nature.'

'I can't imagine what you and I have to talk about.'

'Can't you?'

He walked into the kitchen, shoved a box of potato chips across the floor with his foot to clear his way to a chair, sat at the small chipped table, and waited for Natasha to enter. She came in and sat across from him, placing her hands on the table to disguise the fact that they were shaking. Roche sipped the coffee and set the mug down slowly.

'You always knew how to make a good cup.'

'I don't imagine you've come here to talk about the coffee.'

'I've come here to talk about Theodore.'

'I spoke to your officers. I've said all I have to say.'

'You haven't. Those two don't know what they're doing. I was out of town that day or I would have come here myself, seeing how you and I go back.'

'You and I don't go anywhere, not after what happened.'

'What happened?'

'You know what I'm talking about.'

'The way you moaned meant only one thing.'

'I was in pain. What you did disgusts me.'

Sam got up and walked over to her. He ran his finger across her cheek, then down to her neck.

'Deep down you like it, it excites you to have a man treat you the way you need, just like an animal.'

Natasha stood up and walked away from him.

'Say what you have to say and leave.'

'Who do you think killed Theodore?'

'I don't know.'

'You don't sound like you care.'

'I don't.'

He wagged his finger at her.

'Bad wife.'

'You know the kind of man he was.'

'I know what kind of woman you are,' he said, getting up and moving towards her. She was standing with her back to the door. He pushed her into the wall and ran his hand up her thigh.

'You were always ready for it, weren't you? But you have to put on this act of being better than a whore. It doesn't suit you.'

'You ever touch me again, I'll show you what I am.'

'I think you already did, that time on the floor right here.'

'You raped me, you bastard. You held me down with a fucking knife against my throat.'

'You try telling that to a jury. We were having an affair, one of many in your soiled life. Our sexual games got a little out of hand, that's all. It was a simple mistake.'

'We never had an affair. You just take what you want.'

'It seems to work.'

'I don't know how you were ever born. Your mother must have felt you were a mistake.'

'Like Theodore was a mistake?'

'Like Theodore.'

'Why did you marry him, or was it the money?'

'You think I knew what I was marrying?'

Natasha pulled away and went into the café. She unbolted the door and turned the sign around.

Roche left the kitchen and walked over to the counter. He reached behind it and took a cookie from a dish, broke a piece off, and popped it into his mouth.

'Nice and sweet, just how I like it. I bet you still taste sweet,' he said. 'I've seen those stockings you wear. You like them touching your skin. That gets you real wet. You look good in them, the way you take them off. I've seen the same moves in many a stripper.'

'Theodore told you that, did he?'

'There's a film of you stripping, talking about the rustle

of silk. It makes interesting viewing.'

'He showed you that? I went along with it to stop him hurting me.'

'That's not what he said. He told me you were like a bitch in heat.'

'He threatened to cut me if I didn't perform for him. He said he'd slash my breasts. You did nothing when I came to you. You let me be the prisoner of a sadist, a man who should have been locked up.'

'You're quite dramatic, aren't you? Must be all that sexual tension.'

'Get out.'

'You keep it nice and sweet for me, and I'll be back for dessert.'

'You stay away from me.'

'I'm just doing my duty. Theodore asked me to keep an eye on you.'

'Turn you on, does it? Watching a woman who's been raped forced to strip for her husband.'

'That's your story, like I say, you're a whore.'

'The only pleasure you know is inflicting pain, just like him. I hope he suffered.'

'That right?'

'I wish whoever killed him would come after you.'

'As a police officer I know that a lot of victims lie. It was clear to me that day you lay down on the floor, you'd screw anybody. You were dripping wet.'

'It's a defence mechanism. Don't you know anything about what happens in a woman's body when she's raped?'

'You can't rape a whore. A whore's put herself over a

certain line. You weren't acting on that film. I can still see you peeling off those stockings and moaning.'

'You can fantasise about it all you want, but you ain't ever getting any.'

'A guy like me don't need to fantasise, I got the world at my fingertips.'

'You're just a corrupt cop in a small town who enjoys hurting women.'

'I think you're the corrupt one, a woman with a motive for murdering her husband.'

'Is that what this is about?'

'You were after his money.'

'I don't want his money.'

'That's good. Because Theodore left it all to local business and the police.'

'That doesn't surprise me.'

'You still got the motive.'

'You think I killed Theodore?'

'I know who killed him and so do you.'

'And who might that be?'

'A man named Valentino.'

7.

4:00 p.m.

Patty thought she was being followed after she left The Bounty. An eighteen-wheeler with words HTI on the side lingered outside her hotel. From the opposite side of the street she could see the driver's profile in his wing mirror, his unshaven face, his eyes hidden by reflector shades. He moved on a few feet then stopped again as she walked to the hotel. Patty turned around and headed back to the bar.

Johnny had left, and she mulled over their conversation, ordering another double Jack Daniels. As she sipped it Sam Roche entered the bar.

'What can I get you Sam?' Al said.

'Club soda.'

Al fetched a bottle out of the fridge, opened it, and poured it into a glass.

'No lemon, just ice, right?'

'That's right.'

'I had a journalist in here just now, a guy interested in something to do with missing women.'

'You don't say?'

'I thought maybe he should talk to you.'

'Does this journalist have a name?'

'Yeah, Johnny. Patty, did you catch his second name?'

'I don't believe I did.'

She was sitting a few feet away from them, and up to this point Roche hadn't even looked at her. Now he turned and set his cold eyes on Patty as he sipped his soda.

'Missing women? Can't say I know anything about that,' he said. 'You visiting relatives young lady?'

'No, just passing through.'

Roche nodded and looked away.

'I wanted to ask you if you've seen a man in this bar,' he said to Al, 'unusual looking, kind of exotic, dark hair and eyes, goes by the name Valentino.'

'I can't say I've seen anyone like that,' Al said. 'Is he wanted for something?'

'You could say that. He's the lead suspect in a recent murder. Theodore Mills was killed at a diner up the highway, the one next to the Merchant Stop.'

'Theodore? I can't believe it.'

'I know. It's quite a shock.'

'So this guy Valentino killed him?' Al said.

'That's the premise we're working on. If you see anyone matching his description, call me. Likewise, Patty.' Roche laid his card on the bar in front of her. 'You're in one of the safest parts of the United States. My men watch the highway night and day, and we pick the filth from the road fast.'

After he left, Patty went back to her hotel. She counted out the forty-six dollars she had left. Then she packed, checked out, and walked to the highway. When she got there she thumbed for cars, no trucks. She hitched a ride from a middle-aged woman who smelt of BO and chewed gum all the way to Friskford, where she dropped Patty off.

As Patty wandered down the street looking for accommodation, Valentino was stepping out of the shower at Natasha's house. He was drying himself with a towel when Natasha entered the bathroom.

'I'm worried,' she said.

'About what?'

'I had a visit today from Sam Roche.'

'What did he want?'

'To set you up.'

'For what?'

'Theodore's murder.'

'That's ridiculous.'

'It ain't, not around here. That's why I want us to get away.'

'Why would Sam Roche want to set me up?'

'Because he's got a grudge.'

'Against me?'

'Only indirectly. He wants me, sexually. He did something to me today over at the café, something I don't want to talk about.'

'What?'

'Touched me, in a way I didn't want to be touched, threatened me.'

'He must have spoken to Morgan.'

'I reckon you're right.'

Valentino slipped into some black Jockeys and faded Levis, then put on a crisp blue shirt.

'You're not worried, honey?'

'Why would I worry? I'm innocent.'

'That's not the point. I know what men like Sam Roche are capable of. I've seen things I don't want to talk about.'

'I've heard about Roche's reputation, but I don't think running away is the answer.'

'Why would I want to stay here?'

'What do you think he's going to do, pin some false evidence on me?'

'Maybe. Roche has never met you. I want to get you away from here. If you're not living with me, it'll make it harder for him to find you. You need work, right?'

'You know I do.'

'I know who you can work for, Ronny Simpson. She's an old friend, owns her own bar, Sloppy Joe's, over in Virtue. She'll pay you cash. In the meantime I can sell this place.'

'And what if Roche puts pressure on you?'

'I won't let him find you.'

8.

7:00 p.m.

Friskford was a desolate town. After a brief tour, Patty spotted The Spice Shaker, the local diner. She went inside, ordered a coffee, and read the cards displayed on a board at the back, looking for a local bed and breakfast.

The owner, a sandy-haired woman with freckles, was yawning as Patty ordered a burger from the faded menu.

'How would you like that done?' the owner said, glancing at the clock.

'Medium rare.'

'Any side orders?'

'No.'

'Do you want cheese on your burger?'

'Sure.'

'That it?'

'You know anywhere I can get a bed for a night?'

The owner paused, stared out at the street, then looked at Patty.

'We don't have no hotels here. Suzy used to rent out her son's room, but I don't know if she does anymore.'

'Think it's worth asking?'

She shrugged.

'Maybe.'

'Whereabouts does she live?'

'Second house from the end, other side of the street.'

Patty sat down and sipped her Coke. She calculated she had enough cash for two more nights. When the burger came it was greasy and she covered it in relish. She could see the owner reflected in the window. She was standing with her elbows on the counter and her face in her hands, watching Patty.

She'd almost finished eating when she saw a Jeep pull up in the deserted street. Johnny stepped out and walked into the diner.

'Hello again,' he said.

'I sure am getting that small-town feel.'

'Mind if I join you? I've found out something you might find interesting.'

'Have you? Well I guess I could use some dessert.'

'What will you have?'

'Apple pie, ice cream.'

Johnny ordered a steak sandwich, a coffee, and Patty's pie, then came back and sat opposite her. He leaned across the table and lowered his voice.

'The trucker you talked about, Red, lives here.'

'You mean in Friskford?

'Yes.'

'How did you find this out?'

'I talked to some of the people up at the Merchant Stop. A local businessman was killed there a few nights ago. Red's well-known. He's respected and feared, taken on a lot of big guys in brawls and won, every time, and he's feared because of some of the abuses he's carried out.'

'What abuses?'

'One guy I spoke to said Red had abducted a hooker from the stop and returned her covered in blood.'

'I figured he got his kicks beating up women.'

'Get this, as I was talking to him, a couple of large truckers came up and told me to leave town. I can tell you if I hadn't driven off I think they would have done something.'

The owner put Patty's pie and Johnny's sandwich on the table. Patty dug into the thick crust of pastry with her fork.

'Look, I appreciate you telling me all this, but I have no immediate plans of running into the creep again.'

'I wouldn't stay here.'

'Where do you want me to go? Back to your hotel?'

'That's not what I'm saying.'

She watched Johnny take a bite of the bloodred meat. She ate some vanilla ice cream and stared out of the window at the dark street, feeling cold inside.

'What are you saying, Johnny? Each time I sit down you're sitting right next to me talking about how dangerous it is out there.'

Johnny put his knife and fork down.

'There's an extremely dangerous man out there who's killing women. Do you want to be one of them?'

'I can look after myself.'

She got up and walked to the door.

'It's not me you need to be afraid of,' Johnny said.

He watched her leave the diner and disappear into the darkness.

Patty walked to the end of the street and rang Suzy's bell. There were no lights on in the small peeling house as she peered through the front window. She heard a dog bark at the back. She waited for a few minutes and walked towards the highway, figuring she'd keep moving. She heard a bottle rolling down an alley, and she stopped and saw only shadows. Then she walked out of Friskford. As she stood at the top of the road where the highway blasted past the town, a car drew up.

She couldn't see the driver through the blacked out windows. Then the door opened, and Red got out. Patty began to run, but he was too fast.

He scooped her up in his arms and placed one hand across her mouth, then dragged her back to his car. Her bag lay at the roadside. Patty kicked and struggled, but Red's grip was like a vice. He popped open the trunk of his Honda Crosstour and threw her in.

He peered down at her, his lips wet, his expression feral in the moonlight.

'You got my supper between your legs.'

'Get the fuck away from me. You ain't man enough.'

'I'm animal enough.'

'You him?'

'Who?'

'The maniac trucker. They're all looking for you.'

Red chuckled. He touched her, groped her breasts through her jacket, and shoved his hand between her thighs. Patty kicked him, and he laughed. She listened for the sound of a passing car, but it was as if the town was deserted and she was being offered up as a sacrifice. Then he slammed the trunk shut, and she heard a door close and the engine start. They began to move.

The car picked up speed. Patty tried to steady herself by pushing with her feet against the sides of the trunk, but Red was driving fast and taking corners sharply. The road became uneven after a few miles, and Patty figured they were out beyond the highway. Then suddenly he braked, and she banged her head against the seats.

He got out, and she heard the sound of two male voices.

'What you gonna do?' Red said.

'Over there.'

Silence. Patty's heart hammering in her chest. Then the trunk opened, and she saw Johnny. He was holding a Glock, and it was trained on Red, who was standing a few feet away over by some bushes, his hands behind his head. Patty got out of the trunk as Johnny walked over to Red and held the gun in front of his face.

'Give me one good reason why I shouldn't blow your head off,' he said.

''Cause you ain't got it in you, you're chicken shit.'

Red spat on the ground.

'That's what you think.'

'It's what I know. I seen your type before, rescuing a young thing like that so you can screw her. Come on man, we can take her here, both of us, one end each. You like the sound of that? I tell you there are pleasures to be had in this territory you've never dreamed of.'

'You're a sick man. Now keep walking that way until I don't see you.'

'Or what?'

'I'll shoot.'

'Bullshit.'

Red lowered his arms and moved forward, then Patty

heard the gunshot and saw Red grab his leg.

'Next time it won't be your leg,' Johnny said. 'Now walk.'

Red limped into the bushes. Johnny took the keys to his Honda and threw them in the other direction.

'Get in,' he said to Patty.

She climbed into his Jeep, and he drove away.

'I guess I owe you an apology,' she said.

'You don't know who you can trust out here.'

'How did you know?'

'That he'd abducted you?'

'Yeah.'

'I left the diner after you and made a tour of the area. I saw him throw you in the trunk. I was too far off to stop him, but I tailed him. I'm not following you, Patty. I'm trying to find out what's happening around here.'

'My bag's lying back by the road.'

It began to rain. The drops burst like stars on the black highway as they returned to the place where Red had abducted her. Patty got out of the Jeep and picked up her bag and checked the contents.

'Nothing's missing,' she said.

'I'm not leaving you here. Can I drive you to your hotel?'

'I was going to stay the night in Friskford, but the bed and breakfast doesn't seem to be open anymore.'

'Stay the night at my hotel. I'll sleep on the sofa.'

'You're a true gentleman.'

9.

8:00 a.m.

Patty was asleep when Johnny left the hotel. He bought a coffee from a Shell station and drove to the town of Virtue.

He parked outside a large house surrounded by verdant lawns, situated at the end of the town, a neat parade of well-maintained homes and shops. Johnny rang the bell and waited. An American flag whipped on a polished pole.

An attractive woman with light brown hair that was tied back opened the door. She wore a white blouse and short black skirt and stood there peering at him with the sun in her face.

'How can I help you?'

'I'm looking for Alfred Bennett.'

'And you are?'

'Johnny Sullivan. I'm a journalist.'

'What is this about?'

Johnny saw a tall man in a neat dark blue suit and white shirt approach the door.

'Sonia, it's OK, let the man in,' he said.

Johnny stepped inside the large, immaculately clean hallway.

'Is this about Theodore?' Alfred said.

'Yes and no. I'm sorry to intrude on you like this. I understand he was a business partner.'

'He was, and a good friend. I'm shocked that this has happened.'

'Are you familiar with the Merchant Stop?'

'I've passed through there on occasion.'

'Have you noticed what goes on there?'

'I'm not sure what you mean.'

'I'm talking about the prostitution.'

'At the Merchant Stop?'

'It's packed with prostitutes at night. A large number of women have been abducted in this area. They're being taken from truck stops.'

'Mr. Sullivan, look around you. We live in one of the safest places in the United States. There is no crime here. It's unheard of for an arrest to be made.'

'Don't you find that a little strange?'

'Strange, how?'

'Why do you think Theodore was killed?'

'I have no idea.'

'I'm sorry, Mr. Bennett, I don't mean to grill you. But women are going missing, and I wanted to know if you'd heard anything of the matter.'

'Good heavens, no. Sonia, have you heard about this?'

'I haven't, but I suggest we don't let the coffee get cold. Would you like some, Mr. Sullivan?'

'That would be nice.'

Alfred held out his arm, and Johnny followed Sonia to the kitchen. She was a woman who seemed to be dressing down. She wore no makeup, but her skin was radiant. Johnny guessed she'd been something of a beauty. Alfred was a tanned and handsome man, clean cut, with piercing blue eyes that looked like polished lapis.

They sat at a large wooden table as Sonia poured them a mug each then left.

'Theodore part-owned some of your business, Highway Trucking Incorporated,' Johnny said.

'That's correct.'

'Did he have enemies?'

'Theodore? No, he was extremely well-liked. Although, I have to add, I haven't spoken to him for some months. He was having some personal problems with his marriage.'

'I see.'

'Mr. Sullivan, I'm a little confused as to how I can help you. I know nothing of missing women.'

'I think a trucker's doing it. I thought perhaps you might have noticed suspicious activity.'

'Of what nature?'

'Something in one of your trucks, clothing, blood. How often are they inspected?'

'After every trip, but that's not something I would be involved in. I can assure you that if anything were found it would be reported to the police.'

'Do you have any drivers on your books who have criminal records?'

'Good heavens, no, my drivers are carefully vetted. Would it help if I spoke to the men who carry out the checks and ask them?'

'Yes it would.'

'Then I'd be happy to do so. Do you have a number I can

contact you on?'

'Here's my card.'

'I'll speak to my men and get back to you if there's anything to report.'

'Thank you for your time.'

Alfred showed Johnny to the door and watched him walk to his Jeep. Then he returned to the kitchen where Sonia was making breakfast.

'Should I have told him to leave?' she said.

'No not at all, dear. I don't know what he's after.'

'Strange his coming to your house.'

'I'm happy to help.'

'You're always so understanding of other people.'

'I'm not sure I do understand the nature of his visit.'

As Alfred and Sonia had breakfast, Johnny returned to Purity. Patty was coming out of the bathroom wrapped in a towel, combing her hair when he got back to the room. Her skin looked soft and moist from the shower.

'Sleep well?' he said.

'I did.'

'You want some coffee?'

'I already had some. Where have you been?'

'I got up early. There was someone I wanted to speak to.'

'And you never even touched me.'

After Johnny shot him and drove away, Red stumbled back to his car and called Morgan on his cell phone. Morgan found his keys by the side of the road and took him to a man called Nat Bloomer. He lived in a small one-level house between Scarsdale and Purity. He had trained as a doctor, dropped out before he qualified, and continued to nurse the morphine addiction that had narrowed his life to a single purpose, the continuation of his supply. Truckers used him to stitch up knife wounds from fights, and Red went to him to get his bullet removed.

'Now I wonder who you aggravated this time, Red,' Nat said, as Morgan helped Red inside.

'Just get the fucking thing out.'

'He gets more charming by the day. I bet the ladies love his gentle ways.'

'Nat, do the job and take your money,' Morgan said.

Nat was a small neat man with wiry muscles and cold unmoving eyes. He cut Red's jeans from the wound, shot him with anaesthetic, then inserted a pair of forceps into Red's leg. When he removed them he looked at the dripping bullet with a satisfied grin before he clanked it down on a stainless steel kidney dish.

'Merely a flesh wound,' he said. 'I'll stitch you up.'

'Asshole can't shoot for shit,' Red said.

That morning Red woke in pain, dropped four Advil in his mouth, and made a steak and fried egg breakfast. Then he poured a shot of Jim Beam in a jelly glass and went into his garage, where he got a twenty-two-foot chain and a boat hook. He placed these on the back seat of his Ford E-Series Wagon together with a SIG P220, a knife for filleting fish, some duct tape, and a length of rope, which he tied into a lasso.

There was a look of victory on Red's face as he started the engine and drove to the highway. The scudding clouds looked like torn cotton wool in his blue reflective shades. He was thinking of a woman he once knew, and he could hear her screams beneath the pulsating rhythm of The Rolling Stones song 'Melody' as it blasted out of his dashboard. A warm feeling of well-being consumed him. Red knew it was going to be a good day for him, but probably no one else.

10.

Midday.

Natasha was in her bedroom getting dressed as Valentino sat on the edge of the bed. She was naked, and the light penetrated through a chink in the curtains and graced her full body with even more appeal than it naturally held. Valentino walked over to her and touched her face. Natasha kissed him deeply on the mouth. Then she took his hand and lowered it.

'I'm getting dressed, feeling I'm moving in the wrong direction,' she said. 'It seems to me that naked is best for us, but you gotta go, honey.'

'You're right, time to leave Purity.'

'I'll save you for later. We're gonna take a trip to Virtue, and I'm gonna instruct the local real estate business. You'll be serving beers tonight, and I'll serve my sweet peach to you, covered with thick cream if you like it sweeter than I've given it to you so far.'

'I've no complaints.'

She carried on getting dressed as he packed.

The street felt like a furnace as Patty and Johnny left the Morality Inn. They got into his Jeep, and Johnny drove out of Purity.

'You sure you want to do this?' he said after a few miles.

'Johnny, I appreciate everything you've done for me, but I have things to take care of.'

'What things?'

'They're of a private nature.'

'You think you're safe? You got no money.'

'I've got this far. Red's out of the way.'

'For now.'

'He'll be out of action for a while with a bullet in his leg.'

'I guess there's no persuading you.'

'None at all, I'm not an obedient girl.'

He drove her past Scarsdale and several miles down the highway beyond the next stop and pulled over by the roadside. They got out and stood in the blazing sun. Johnny reached into his pocket, took out his wallet, and handed her a hundred dollars.

'You're gonna need some cash.'

'You don't need to give me more than you already have.'

'I haven't given you anything.'

'You gave me respect last night. That's worth more than dollars to me.'

'Come on, take it. And stay out of trouble.'

'I'll stay out of Friskford if that's what you mean. I know you mean to help, but I have to do this on my own.'

'What is it you want to do?'

'I'm trying to find someone.'

'Who?'

Patty hesitated, stared down the empty highway, then

turned her dark brown eyes on him.

'My sister, Daisy. She disappeared some time back. I know you're straight Johnny, but I need to find her on my own, she won't trust no one else.'

'Where do you think she is?'

'I don't know, maybe hooking, maybe worse.'

'I could help you find her.'

'Thank you for saving my life, but maybe it ain't worth saving.'

'Don't talk like that.'

'I'll be seeing you.'

'Will you?'

'Good-bye, Johnny.'

She leaned up and kissed him on the cheek, then turned away and walked along the highway, a diminutive figure in faded jeans. Johnny stood there, staring after her, then got in his Jeep and turned it around and aimed it for Purity, his heart heavy in his chest, his eyes wet, the road a blur beneath his spinning wheels.

Patty walked a mile and stopped to sip some water. The sun was blinding, and she sat by the roadside on an old log and smoked a cigarette. The undergrowth beyond the road was thick, trash hung from a few branches, plastic potato chip wrappers and a fading Zinger packet, remnants of roadside snacks. A condom was draped over a flat tire, and a bleached dog's skull sat in the dust. Patty was looking at it, wondering how it got there, when she heard tires screech behind her. She turned to see Red getting out of his wagon with a rope in his hand.

'Well, well, if it ain't little miss snatch,' he said.

Patty began to run, but Red whipped the lasso through

the dry air and caught her around the neck. He pulled her onto her back and dragged her to his wagon. He leant down and pressed the filleting knife to her throat.

'I've fucked more bitches than I care to remember, and you're next.'

Patty tried to kick him between the legs, but she couldn't reach.

'You can kick all you want, but my big old dick's gonna be sliding inside you in a few minutes and then the look of pleasure on your face will say it all.'

She was choking, and spittle ran down her chin.

'You want to scream? No one's gonna hear you out here, not on this stretch of highway. I know every inch of it, same way I'm gonna know every inch of your body before I cut it up and ready it for what happens next. This is my country, this is my highway. You're gonna scream for me when I get you there.'

He slung her in the back of his wagon like a side of beef, and she landed on the chain. She was winded and gasping for breath. Red let go of the rope, and she pulled it free from her neck.

'I hooked that up to a whore one summer, placed the hook deep inside her sorry snatch and dragged her along on the chain all the way to the state line. You could say she had a fulfilling experience reaching a climax she'd never imagined possible. What do you think about that?'

'Fuck you,' Patty said, getting to her feet.

'It's gonna be the other way around,' Red said, climbing in. 'I'm gonna use you and spit you out, bitch. You're in the wrong town.'

'There are plenty of hookers out there, why are you hunting me down?

'I never fail to deliver my cargo.'

'Where were you taking me the other night?'

'You'll find out.'

He punched her hard in the stomach. Patty rolled over onto her side, gagging. Red picked her bag up from the road and threw it in after her.

'Don't want to leave any evidence behind, do we?'

'They'll find you.'

'They won't.'

'You're a big man ain't you? I bet the bullet hurt.'

'Nothing I ain't felt before. But you're gonna feel some things you'll never want to feel again.'

He locked the door and drove away.

11.

6:00 p.m.

Sloppy Joe's was located half way down Main Street in Virtue. Ronny Simpson had run the bar for twelve years and took pride in delivering a good service to her customers, mostly locals who came to idle away the hours when they didn't want to be home. Ronny would sometimes drink with them and always kept their confidences when they poured out their troubles, whether they were of a marital nature or something darker. That was why, she said, she did good business, because people knew she didn't talk behind their backs. It was an inconsistency in a woman who saw little good in the world, mistrusted others, and drank heavily. She'd usually be seen in her bar with a martini or vodka in her hand.

She was an attractive woman on whom the years showed like an angry imprint of disappointment and hidden resentments. There was hardness in her features, and she often narrowed her eyes when she spoke. She was full-figured and liked to show her cleavage in cocktail dresses and bend across the bar as she talked to the regulars, with whom she never slept. That was one rule Ronny held, never sleep with the locals.

That evening the sky was the colour of a blood orange

as Valentino stepped out of Natasha's black Chrysler and walked up to Sloppy Joe's. Ronny saw him from the bar, his white shirt a brilliant glare against his toned chest. She poured herself an Absolut as she waited for them to enter and brushed a speck of dust from her black satin skirt.

When they did, she paid attention to Natasha, not acknowledging Valentino.

'Well, how are you?' she said, walking over and kissing Natasha on the cheek.

'Pretty well.'

'I heard about Theodore. It must be hard all the same.'

'Hard? You know how he was.'

'Sure. What a way to go.'

'Ronny, thanks for seeing us at such short notice.'

'Any time. Can I get you a drink?'

'This is Valentino.'

'Well, pleased to meet you,' Ronny said, extending her hand and allowing her gaze to linger on his eyes and mouth.

'Wine, right?' she said to Natasha.

'I better not.'

'Come on.'

'Just a glass, then.'

'Valentino, what's your pleasure?'

'I'll have a Bloody Mary.'

She poured Natasha a chilled pinot grigio and made a double Bloody Mary for Valentino, shaking in some Worcestershire sauce and Tabasco, then ground pepper from a large wooden mill. She set the drinks down on a table at the back and watched Valentino sip from his glass.

'Good?'

'Extremely,' Valentino said. 'It has quite a kick to it.'

Natasha sipped her wine.

'Oh, this is nice.'

'All the way from Oregon,' Ronny said. 'Now I hear you're looking for bar work, Valentino.'

'That's right.'

'Done any before?'

'Many times.'

'Whereabouts?'

'All over.'

'Think you know your way around some of the more obscure Arizona drinks?'

'I know my way around many obscure things, try me.'

'All right, fix me a Barry Goldwater.'

She and Natasha watched as Valentino went behind the bar, got the berry and acai vodka and Bertagnolli mirtillo grappa, Encanto pisco and lemon juice, and blackberries and sage from the fridge and mixed it up, moving quickly, fluidly, serving it on ice. He placed it on the bar and watched as Ronny strode over and sipped it.

'Not bad,' she said, wagging a finger at him. 'Next up, a Gin Blossoms.'

Valentino got the gin and Martini.

When he served it to her she took a sip and said, 'You're hired.'

'I told you he was good,' Natasha said.

'Not that many customers ask for these drinks. I just thought I'd put your man to the test.'

Ronny looked immaculate as she stood there in her indigo blouse and tight skirt. She took out a cigarette, and

Valentino lit it for her.

'I believe you have a small place above the bar where he can stay,' Natasha said, suddenly nervous.

12.

Midnight.

Sam Roche unchained the Dobermans and led them out into the moonlight. Their ribcages showed like steel bars beneath their slick black fur. A thin cigar smouldered in his mouth as his eyes darted across the landscape, sharp pinpoints of hatred scanning his territory.

After a few minutes he went back into his house and fed the dogs from a bowl they fought over. Then he went upstairs where his wife Sandra was brushing her hair in their bedroom.

'Sam, have you been outside?' she said.

'There was a noise in the garden. I thought it was an intruder.'

'There was no one there?'

'No.'

'Coming to bed?'

'In a while. I have some papers to look at, there's some business I have to attend to that might take me out of state.'

Sandra was a pretty woman, whose eyes were filled with repressed fear and seemed to only hold one expression. She had a pale, unlined face and a full sensuous mouth that didn't seem to belong to her. Her attractiveness was overshadowed by sadness. She bore the look of a deep sorrow that made her seem older than her years. Roche watched as she got into bed, took a sleeping pill, and put the light out, then turned her back to him and shut her eyes. He sat there for an hour counting the minutes pass on the digital clock by the bed, waiting for her to fall into a deep sleep, watching the sheets rise and fall with her breathing, his eyes unblinking, then he went downstairs into the garage.

A pile of boxes covered an entire wall, and Roche began to remove them. Behind them was a safe buried deep in the stone. Roche opened it and removed what looked like a piece of fur. Then he took some zip ties from a metal drawer full of rusting nails, got in his dark blue Buick and drove out into the night. He might have described the thoughts that accompanied him on his nocturnal visit as consoling in nature. But the things that brought Sam Roche consolation were not of the kind that many men would find solace in. They consisted of a series of images, seemingly disconnected. They involved dismemberment and pain and his face laughing beneath a moon.

Natasha was lying in bed unable to sleep when he drew up a few houses away. She didn't hear him shut his engine off. She was thinking about Ronny and Valentino and whether Ronny would try to get Valentino into bed. She'd left them at around seven and spent the evening making plans to sell the house.

She began to doze, as Roche walked up her path, inserted a card into her door and entered her darkened hallway. Then he put on the mask. He'd cut the wolf's head from a lupine skull one murderous night whose intensity left him with a memory of arousal he was constantly trying to find in extreme acts that had no place in his marriage. As he stood in

Natasha's house he began to feel it stir inside him. The night was full of smells to Roche as he climbed her stairs. He was fully aroused by the time he got to Natasha's bed.

Natasha thought she was dreaming when she saw the wolf enter her bedroom. Then she screamed.

What happened next would always be a blur that induced nausea in her. The man wearing the wolf's head cut her night clothes from her body with a pair of scissors while he held her down by the throat. Then he began to touch her. It all seemed to happen in dream sequence. She was gasping for air, her body soaked in sweat as he tied her to the bed with the zip ties, lashing them around her wrists, forcing her legs apart, and shackling her ankles to the bed posts.

He released his grip, let her breathe, and slammed his hand down on her mouth. Then he reached inside his pocket and removed a pair of stockings and gagged her with one of them, tying it so hard around her mouth she tasted blood. He placed the other stocking between her legs. Then he leant down and pressed the wolf's muzzle against her face, as if he was going to eat it.

Roche was silent as he assaulted Natasha, pausing in his violation only to say these words, 'I can smell things other men can't. I smell it on you. Gift from Theodore, whore.'

Natasha felt paralysed for much of the assault. A part of her brain shut down when he entered the room, as if what was happening was not real. Now she began to struggle, but as she writhed beneath Roche in the wolf's head it excited him. As she pulled on the zip ties they tightened, cutting her circulation off.

Roche unzipped his fly and got on top of her. He ran the stocking across her nipples then he pulled a serrated knife from his coat. He placed it between her legs, stroking the edge against her thigh. He parted her lips with his fingers. His hard penis lay on her leg as she felt something cold touch her vagina.

Then another figure entered the room. Natasha couldn't see this other person, but she saw her assailant turn. As she did she felt the cold object move away from her genitals.

Her attacker fell away from her. The figure behind him was holding a Taser against his neck. Then she heard the sound of two muffled gunshots, and her hands were freed. She tried to see the face of the man who saved her as he cut the zip ties loose with a knife, but he was wearing a hood low across his face. Then she was alone in the room with the body and the wolf's head.

She stood up and collapsed. She was lying in blood and pulled herself back onto the bed and stared down at the man on her carpet. She pulled the wolf's head off and looked at Sam Roche's face. His eyes were open, and he looked more feral than the wolf. He was holding her stocking in his hand. There was a smell like canine urine in the room and Natasha began to gag. She inspected herself, putting her hand between her legs. She wasn't cut, but there were globules of cold semen clinging to her thighs.

13.

2:00 a.m.

Marshall Simmons brushed a speck of dust from the arm of the shabby sofa in the rundown house that stared at the derelict railway track. Renee Jenkins was making him a late snack, and the clock ticked by as he stared out of the window at the shadows in the overgrown garden, dressed in a pair of filthy grey trousers and a vest with a hole that looked like a cigarette burn at the back. His right arm sported a tattoo of a naked woman.

He ran his greasy hand across his stubble, then put a finger into his mouth, and spat something he found lodged between his teeth onto the floor before walking through the hallway into the kitchen. He stood there and stared at Renee's back.

She was dressed in a bright green skirt, white stilettos, and a silver blouse that was too tight. She was an attractive woman, in her early twenties. She had dark brown hair and sparkling green eyes that shone out of her tanned face. She brushed a tear from one eye and looked out of the window, at the empty night, desolation catching in her throat, before she saw Marshall's reflection in the glass and stopped. She turned around as he walked over to her and inspected the food she was preparing.

'I hope you're making it better than last time,' he said.

'It's Spam.'

'I know that, but the rest of it.'

'What about it, what's wrong with it?'

'That tomato looks wrong.'

'Wrong, how?'

'As wrong as you.'

Renee stood there with the knife in her hand, waiting for him to say more, then he laughed, patted her behind, and said, 'Get changed, and we can have a cup of tea. Reminds me of sausage meat.'

'What does?'

'Your legs inside those tights, get them off.'

Renee carried on chopping tomatoes. He laid his hand on her shoulder and turned her around.

'You heard what I said.'

'Why does it have to be this way?'

'You know why.'

'What kind of life is this?'

'Nice house. You're free.'

'Am I?'

'What do you think?'

'Why do you need to be like this?'

'I like animals, Renee.'

Renee laid the cheap green plates on the chipped table, set the salad bowl down, then the Best Foods mayonnaise, which had congealed at the top and turned brown. She put four slices of Spam on Marshall's plate. Then she boiled the kettle and made a pot of tea which she set before him in a tea cosy in the shape of a cow.

'That what you want me to be?' she said, pointing at it.

'It's not a cow day today.'

'What then?'

'You'll see.'

Marshall poured himself a cup of tea.

'Why do you talk like that? Pretend you're not American?' she said.

'I'm whatever I want to be.'

'You sound like a Brit.'

'What do you know about it? You don't even know who you are anymore.'

'That's because you've taken it away.'

'What?'

'Who I am, you've abducted her and left me here with this.'

'You should count yourself lucky you're a pet. Some animals get locked in cages and starved.'

'Pet?'

'Plenty of meat on your bones.'

'Why do you want all this tea?'

'Not good enough for you, is it? Ever felt how hot a cup of tea is when poured down your nipples?'

'We're not in Britain, this is America.'

'How do you know where we are?'

'I hear the trucks sometimes.'

Marshall jabbed his forefinger at her.

'You think you do.'

'I hear them beyond the railway track. They're always going somewhere.'

'I'm going to be generous. You can keep one item on. Start at the top.'

'Aren't you going to put the music on?'

'After I've eaten, then I'm going to give you a present.'

'What?'

'An item of jewellery that I think will suit you nicely.'

Renee unbuttoned her blouse slowly, glancing out of the window.

'Look at me as you do it,' Marshall said.

She did as she was told. She put the blouse on the chair, then unhooked her bra, and laid that down too. Marshall looked at her standing there waiting for his instructions. She folded her arms across her breasts.

'Arms by your side, the rest.'

She unzipped her skirt slowly, pulled it down, then removed her tights, placing one leg then the other on the chair, looking at Marshall.

'This enough?'

'You can keep the shoes on.'

She lowered her G-string and stood there waiting.

Marshall got up and inspected her. She raised her arms and he looked at her armpits, then ran his fingers across her nipples, and said, 'Good.'

'I stopped shaving as you asked,' she said.

'So you're dark haired, the way I like it.'

'I don't dye my hair.'

'I'll have a drink.'

Marshall sat down and Renee pressed her large breasts into his face and he chewed on her nipples as she bit her lip.

'Not too hard,' she said.

'I want some fucking milk, bitch.'

Marshall pushed as much of each breast as he could into his mouth and sucked hard, then he sat back, and wiped his mouth.

'Let's eat,' he said.

Renee sat on the chair wearing only her high heels and poked at the Spam and tomato salad as Marshall chewed loudly. When he'd finished he pushed his chair back and belched. Renee laid her knife and fork down and stood up. Marshall looked at her and motioned to the heels.

'Off with the lot, it's party time,' he said.

'How much longer does this have to go on?'

'Get dressed in the outfit, and I'll get my gloves.'

Renee went upstairs to the cramped bedroom while Marshall walked through to the living room, opened an old turntable, and put on *The Best of ABBA*. He went into the hall and took a pair of surgical gloves out of a cupboard. He nudged the plastic firmly between his fingers, then returned to the living room where he sat in a green chair with a sunken seat and waited.

As 'Waterloo' played, Renee entered the room wearing a small fur coat that stopped at her waist.

'Open it,' Marshall said.

'Is this all you want me to wear?'

Marshall stood up.

'I'll give you the other thing you need.'

He opened a drawer and removed a dog leash.

'On your knees,' he said.

Renee undid the fur coat and got down onto the stained carpet, placing her hands, and knees a few feet apart. Marshall sat on her back and placed the chain around her neck and yanked hard. Her head tilted back, and her eyes bulged as she choked. Then he slapped her backside and said, 'Walk.' Renee began to crawl across the carpet, struggling with Marshall's weight before collapsing by the door. Marshall stood up and said, 'Dance.'

Renee got to her feet and danced awkwardly to ABBA, the chain swinging against her breasts. It was hurting her, and she moved it.

'I touch the leash, not you,' Marshall said.

He walked over to her, removed the fur coat, and took hold of the chain in his clenched fist.

When she finished, he said, 'You can get dressed now.'

He removed his surgical gloves as she went into the kitchen. When she came back into the living room she was crying.

'Why do you have to keep doing this?' Renee said.

'Don't you like a party?'

'These aren't parties.'

'What do you call them then?'

'I don't call them anything.'

'We have music and dancing. You enjoy yourself. You said you like dressing up.'

'Not as an animal.'

'You think you're better than them?'

'When are you going to let me see my baby?'

'Be a pet, Renee.'

Marshall picked his gloves up and put them back on. He punched Renee hard in the stomach and watched as she doubled over, saliva stringing from her mouth.

She straightened up and caught her breath. Marshall

grabbed her left arm and jabbed at the track marks that ran across her veins like angry insect bites.

'Why are you doing this to me?' she said.

'Time for your fix.'

'Who am I?'

'You're Renee, and just you remember that.'

14.

4:00 a.m.

Some of them wore dog's heads, some the heads of wild cats. The hookers were screaming.

In a yard stained with moonlight, the men began cutting the women. They used machetes and long-handled knives. A large figure wearing the head of a cougar lifted a small prostitute in a red miniskirt off the ground and severed her neck in a short motion with a butcher's knife, spraying blood onto the man next to him. A muscular figure in a coyote's head chopped casually at a woman with an axe. Then they began to howl. It was a slow metronomic noise that pierced the night and reached beyond the wasteland where they'd gathered to the hissing highway where trucks sped towards their morning destinations while the men in masks carried out their nocturnal rituals.

The women were mutilated, some of them decapitated. The men carried their bodies to a large truck that was parked at the edge of the area and placed them inside. Then they left the area in a convoy.

After she'd showered the stain that was Sam Roche

from her body, Natasha poured herself a cognac and called Valentino. He sounded groggy as he answered.

'Natasha?'

'Honey, I'm coming to pick you up, I need you here.'

'What's happened?'

'I've been attacked.'

Valentino got out of bed, dressed, and left the small room above Sloppy Joe's and waited by the door until Natasha pulled up outside. When she saw him she got out of her car and threw her arms around him and began to shake. Valentino held her and then drove back to Purity as she told him what had happened.

Sam Roche's body still lay on the bedroom floor.

'I'm going to bury him,' Valentino said. 'That pond you were building at the end of the garden, the hole's several feet deep.'

He went into the garage and fetched a sheet of tarpaulin. He rolled the body inside it and carried it down to the garden. He stopped at the end near the wall and put the body down.

'We can't be seen here,' he said.

As the men in animal masks were killing the hookers, Valentino was burying Sam Roche. He sliced the spade into the ground, digging deep into the ditch. The only sound he and Natasha heard as he dug was the engine of a truck being silenced somewhere in Purity, and Valentino stopped in his exertions for a few seconds to listen, both of them wondering who was returning home at that time. Dawn was breaking as he laid Sam Roche in the ground and covered him up, smoothing the soil on top.

Then he and Natasha removed the carpet in the bedroom and washed the walls, cleaning it with bleach.

They lay down in the spare room as light streamed through the curtains.

They rose at midday, and Natasha showered with him. She made breakfast and watched Valentino eat.

'What do we do with the carpet?' she said.

'I know a place where I can burn it.'

'Do you think I should replace it?'

'Leave it. I think the tiles look good.'

That afternoon Valentino drove to a disused building near a truck stop, pulling up by what had been a gas station. Natasha stared at the rusting pumps and the trash drifting across the oil-stained ground in the light breeze as he opened the trunk and removed the carpet, which he'd wrapped it in several layers of plastic sheeting. He carried it to a building beyond the pumps. Then he went inside. He was gone for some time, and when he returned he was sweating.

'How do you know about this place?' Natasha said.

'I drove past it once, looking for gas.'

'What's in there?' she said, motioning to the building with her head.

'An incinerator.'

'Oh, is that all?'

'I've heard there used to be a farm back here. The farmer burned sick animals in it.'

She drove him to Sloppy Joe's, and then she went to see the real estate agents. That day she put her house on the market.

15.

The police got a call the next day about an arm that had been found near a section of highway beyond Purity. The hand bore the tattoo of a woman in chains and an animal.

Officers Harry Reed and Mitch Samuels cordoned off the section of highway, and inspected the limb that lay in the dust, the sun beating down on their backs. It was a right arm that had been hacked roughly at the elbow. The bone jutted through the severed skin and the flesh was ragged where it had been cut. Reed scratched his head.

'What do you make of the tattoo, Mitch?' he said.

'I seen it before, Harry.'

'Yeah? So who's the owner?'

'I do believe that arm belongs to Red.'

'The trucker? You serious?'

'I ain't ever seen a tattoo like it elsewhere.'

'What sort of animal is that?'

'I never did figure it out, but I pulled Red in once for questioning about a rape. I kept staring at that thing trying to figure out what it is, kind of nasty ain't it?'

'Sure is, it looks like a wolf.'

'I'll call it in. I'm sure Roche will want to know about this.'

'He doesn't strike me as the kind of man who wants to get tangled up in a missing limb.'

'Normally I'd say you're right, Harry, but that time I pulled Red in, I had enough on him to hold him. He'd been seen with the woman shortly before she was found by the roadside pretty beat up, and she'd been raped. All the evidence was there. Roche stormed into the station and ordered me to release him.

'How's that?'

'Said he could personally account for Red's whereabouts. What do you say to that?'

'What happened to the woman?'

'I don't know. She disappeared.'

Samuels put the call through as Reed spoke to the driver of another police car that was drawing up. When Reed walked back, Samuels was starting the engine of their vehicle.

'Deputy Director Norman wants to see us,' he said.

'Why?'

'Beats me.'

'I need a Coke.'

Samuels drove back to the station, pulling over at a truck stop on the way there. Reed climbed out of the car, wiped the sweat from his brow, and leaned in.

'Get you anything, Mitch?'

'Na, I think I'm all right.'

Reed went into the small shop, got a large Coke and some barbecue-flavoured chips, then stood in line. A large trucker was leaning across the counter. A plump woman whose blouse was open at the top bent and got something out of a box, as he eyed her cleavage. He paid and walked away, stopping a few feet from Reed as he slapped another trucker on the shoulder.

'Hey Burt, how you doing?' the trucker said.

'Morgan, didn't see you there, buddy, pretty good.'

'You should have been there the other night.'

'Had a little business to take care of out of state otherwise, you know.'

Morgan laughed and they shook hands. The line inched forward, and Reed paid then got back in the car.

As Reed and Samuels stood in front of Deputy Director Franklin Norman they sensed tension surrounding their finding. Norman was a man who normally had little to do with officers of a lesser rank and who worked closely with Sam Roche. He and Roche went back years, when they'd both been prison guards in another state. Norman was six one, had a neatly trimmed black moustache, on which there was never a hair out of place, and the flexed muscularity of a military physique. He had short dark hair and unsettling eyes. The left one was mantis green, and the right one black, as if two men inhabited him. When he looked at his officers, they felt he knew something about their record they didn't have access to.

'What are your findings?' Norman said.

'A severed right arm on the highway, we believe it belongs to a trucker named Red,' Samuels said.

Norman walked over to them.

'Why do you think that?'

'The tattoo on his hand,' Samuels said. 'I seen it before when I pulled him in once.'

'That right?'

'Yes, Sir.'

'And you, Reed, what do you think?'

'I've never seen the tattoo before, Sir.'

'We got forensics running tests. I'll take over from here.'

'We'll write our report,' Reed said.

'Put it on my desk.'

'Not Director Roche's?'

'Not Director Roche's, I'm dealing with this investigation.'

Fifteen minutes later Norman left the station in his car. He drove to Red's house, parked, put on a pair of plastic gloves, got some forensic bags out of his trunk, and walked up the path. The front door was open, and Red's wagon was parked at an angle on the drive, the passenger door ajar.

Norman drew his SIG P226 and went into the house. The first room on the left of the hall was a mess. Drawers lay open, some turned over on the floor, clothes and various objects scattered everywhere. Several copies of *Hustler* lay among them. Norman went into the kitchen where an empty bottle of Jim Beam sat on a table in a shaft of sunlight. The counters were smeared with grease, and the room smelled of fried steak and sweat. He went upstairs and stood in the hallway, off which there were two rooms with their doors shut.

In the first one was a bed with a pair of yellow cami knickers and a deep-blue, bloodstained G-string on it. The cami knickers had a tear in them that Norman identified as a knife cut. He went into the second room, opening the door slowly. It was dark in there, the curtains drawn. Norman couldn't make out the shape on the bed, so he turned on the light.

Red's head sat in a dried pool of blood that was as dark as his faded black sheets. The rest of him lay on the carpet next to the bed, his left hand clutching a Luger, his right shoulder a stump. He had multiple wounds.

Norman went downstairs and inspected Red's wagon. It was empty, apart from the chain he took with him when he abducted Patty. Norman went back into the house. He found a set of keys on a table in the hall. He looked at each of the keys, selected one and went out to Red's garage. He unlocked it and walked inside, closing the door and pulling the cord on the light.

There was a workbench at the rear of the garage, and he pulled it away from the wall. Behind it was a safe which Norman opened. He began removing some boxes from it. He put these in the trunk of his car, locked the garage, placed the keys back in the hall and drove away. That afternoon he told two detectives to inspect the murder scene.

16.

Ronny asked Valentino to share a drink with her after work. They'd had a busy night. She lit a candle and put a bottle of tequila on a table at the back, beneath the painting of the woman who decorated the matches that sat in large glass bowls on either end of the bar. Ronny was wearing a short black skirt and a beige blouse with clearly no bra underneath it. She was a little drunk. She poured them both a double shot and rubbed her neck.

'Are you any good with your hands?' she said.

'Do you feel tense?'

'Yeah, I feel tense all over. I'm sure you can help me with that.'

'I can.'

Valentino sipped his tequila.

'I'm not asking you to do it to me naked.'

'Where are you stiff?' he said, standing up and coming behind her.

He began to knead her shoulders gently, then applied firmer pressure.

'I could tell,' she said.

'What?'

'That you'd have the touch.'

'Maybe another drink,' he said, sitting down and reaching for the bottle.

'Fill my glass for me,' she said, holding it up. 'Do I make you nervous?'

'No.'

'You could carry on.'

'Maybe I need to go to bed.'

'On your own?'

'Ronny.'

'How come?'

'How come what?'

'You and Natasha?'

'She's an attractive woman.'

'Yes, and so am I.'

'I work for you.'

'And what if you weren't working for me?'

'I think that's the wrong question.'

'What's the right question?'

'It's not the job that would stand in the way.'

'But Natasha.'

Valentino tipped the rest of his drink into his mouth.

'Good night.'

'You know, there are things about her you may not like.'

'I think it's been a long day.'

'The nights are long.'

'Thank you for the drink.'

'You know her husband was a pretty bad dude.'

'I heard.'

'Natasha knew all about that but stayed with him, ever wonder why?'

'Some people become prisoners.'

'Is that what you think?'

'I think there's too much trouble in this conversation.'

'Trouble? That's funny. You stand out, Valentino. Look around you at the other men hereabouts, they don't know about women, but you do, and you pick Natasha.'

'You think that's how it happened?'

'I don't know, but I do know Natasha.'

'And so do I.'

'What do you know?'

'Enough.'

Ronny stood up and walked over to him.

'How did a man like you end up here? This place is full of truckers.'

'I found it off the highway.'

Ronny watched him walk to the door that led up to his room.

Johnny was about to go to sleep when a call came through on his cell phone.

'I'm outside the hotel, I need a place to stay for the night,' Patty said.

A few minutes later she was in his room. She looked dirty, her hair was unkempt, and she had a black eye and a cut lip.

'What happened to you?' Johnny said.

'You were right. I shouldn't have gone off on my own. Red came after me, beat me up, he was going to kill me.'

'How did you get away?'

'Someone saved my life.'

'Who?'

'I don't know. I didn't see them, a figure with a hood low down over his face. He told me to get out of there.'

Johnny went over to her and put his arms around her.

'No more hitchhiking, Patty.'

'You got it, Johnny.'

'You hungry? I got some pizza in the box. It's cold.'

'I don't care if it's frozen.'

He watched Patty sit on the chair and eat. Then she went into the bathroom and ran a bath. When she came out Johnny was dozing off on the sofa. She put her hand on his arm.

'You don't have to sleep down there,' she said.

'It's pretty hard. I think you need the bed.'

'It's big enough for both of us.'

'You don't have to feel bad. I'm just glad you're all right.'

She was standing at the back of the sofa, and he looked up at her. She was naked and went over to the bed, and Johnny got up. She turned the sheets back. He looked at her full body as she lay down and her dark hair as it spread across the white pillow, and he thought how beautiful she was. Then he got in with her, and Patty pulled him towards her.

17.

9: 00 a.m.

'So who do you think saved you?' Johnny said.

'Like I said, I couldn't see his face, but Red had enemies, that's for sure.'

Patty was sitting on the bed in one of Johnny's T-shirts. She had her legs crossed and her ankles tucked under her. They were drinking coffee. Sunlight drifted into the room through a crack in the curtains.

'You remember what you told me, about the time he picked you up and you got away? He mentioned a madman who attacked a woman.'

'He ate a woman's face, according to Red, although he may have been describing himself. Who knows what he had in store for me or what games he was playing with me?'

'Did this man have a name?'

'Donald Lake.'

'You know, it sounds familiar.'

'He must have made it up, why would he have told me it?'

'Because he thought he had you trapped and you weren't going to be repeating it.'

'Maybe.'

'Where was this meant to have taken place?'

'Massachusetts. Red said he used to be a psychiatric nurse.'

Patty sipped her coffee.

'This doesn't taste right,' she said.

'It's fresh.'

'Nothing tastes right out here. It's as if I'm living in an ersatz world. I stepped off the highway into some other place. You know, people have told me I ain't in Arizona. Sometimes I think I've drifted into Mexico. Johnny, do you believe there are places off the map?'

'I think we've mapped too much of the world.'

'But what if, the same with the rain forests and the oceans, there are parts of the States that we don't know about, at least not through maps or the media?'

'I think we're spied on. I think the authorities know just about all there is to know, through satellite and the internet.'

'What if there are parts they don't know about?'

'Someone would find out.'

'Someone like us?'

Later that morning Johnny went to the truck stop up the highway from Virtue. Morgan was standing by his truck eating a hot dog, the yellow mustard squirting out of the side as Johnny walked up.

'Want something?' Morgan said.

'I was wondering if I could ask you some questions.'

''Bout what?'

'Missing women.'

'Your old lady run off?'

'I thought you might have seen something.'

'I seen a lot of things.'

'I believe someone is abducting women.'

'Do you? I didn't get your name.'

'Johnny.'

'I don't know nothing about no missing women.'

'What do they call you?'

'Morgan. Now, I got a truck to drive.'

Morgan screwed up the paper napkin that held his hot dog and began to walk away.

'You a friend of Red's?'

Morgan stopped, his back to Johnny, then he turned around and walked over, looking down his barrel of a chest at him. Deep blue veins ran across his thick neck.

'Why d'you wanna know?'

'Just asking.'

Morgan stared at Johnny, then turned his head and spat.

'That right?'

He walked away and got in his truck. Johnny went into the café and ordered a coffee. He sat in his Jeep and drank it, then he drove back to Purity.

As he was nearing the town a blue pickup came up fast behind him. The driver began to flash him, then overtook him, and slammed on his brakes, forcing Johnny to stop. He hit the rear bumper of the pickup. Two men got out, one of them Morgan. The other man had the pumped iron look of a body builder. Johnny flipped open the glove compartment, pulled out a Glock and stuck it in the back of his jeans. Morgan opened the driver's door of Johnny's Jeep and turned off the ignition.

'Get out,' he said.

'What's this about?'

'You heard him,' the other man said.

Johnny went and stood near the back of his Jeep.

'You ask too many questions,' Morgan said, jabbing his finger at Johnny's chest.

'Why would it matter to you?'

'Where do you come from, boy?' the other man said.

'The truck stop up the highway.'

'Don't get smart,' Morgan said.

'I'm going to get in my Jeep now. I think this conversation's over.'

'Do you?'

'That's what I said.'

'Burt, grab his arms.'

Johnny reached into the back of his belt and pulled his Glock.

'Get in your pickup and drive away,' he said.

'Maybe you're behind the missing people.'

Morgan pulled a knife.

'I'm gonna cut you,' he said, walking towards Johnny.

Johnny fired a shot at Morgan's feet, stopping him in his tracks. Burt had edged around the back of the Jeep, and Johnny spun around and shot so close to Burt's cowboy boots he showered them with dirt.

'We ain't finished with you, boy,' Morgan said.

They got in their pickup and drove away.

When Johnny got back to the Morality Inn he told Patty what had happened and what Morgan had said about Red.

'Well I reckon they're all working together,' she said.

'Then the abductions are the work of more than one man, there is no maniac trucker.'

18.

1:00 p.m.

Renee Jenkins stood in the bathroom and looked at herself in the mirror. Her attractive face was marked by stress. And the heroin was taking its toll.

'I don't want to be Renee anymore,' she said.

She put on some tight black slacks and a violet blouse, a pair of white shoes and a gold belt that she fastened tightly around her waist. She went downstairs and looked at Marshall's collection of surgical gloves. They lay neatly piled in a drawer beneath his collection of ABBA records. Then she heard the numerous locks sliding open on the door, and Marshall walked in from the hallway.

'I didn't expect you back,' she said.

'I can see that.' He took off his baseball cap and placed it on the chair. 'Do you really think I'd leave you unchained for long?'

'You've only been gone a few minutes.'

'Now what have you been up to?'

'I haven't been up to anything.'

He came over to her and put his hands on her breasts.

'Do you want to eat something, Marshall?'

'Yes.'

'I meant some food.'

'That's what it is, isn't it?'

Renee began to sweat as Marshall unbuttoned her blouse and took it off. Beneath the single bulb that dangled from the ceiling he lowered her slacks and pulled down her G-string.

'I think it's time for a party.'

'I haven't done anything.'

'Then you can show me that, can't you? I'm a fair man.'

'Is it fair to do this to me? I want to see my baby.'

'Do you want to know what the law does to mothers like you, to drug addicts?'

He went into the hall and came back with a dog's head. He held a leash in his other hand.

'You want to see her?' he said.

'You know I do.'

'Then you have to learn that you're an animal, now put it on.'

Renee stared at the animal mask and placed it over her head. She could hear 'Take a Chance on Me' playing as she felt his plastic gloves slide across her flesh.

'Kneel,' he said.

She bent her knees and reached out into the darkness until she felt the carpet beneath her hands.

All she could hear was the music. Then she felt Marshall enter her from behind. He inserted his penis deep inside her and leaning on her said, 'Walk.'

Renee crawled across the floor as he worked his way to his violent release. As she heard him groan he wrapped the dog leash around her throat and pulled until she was gasping and her body tightened. She clenched hard on his penis and Marshall said, 'That's how I like it, just like a fox. I knew what kind of animal you were the first time I set eyes on you. You belong in a cage.'

She collapsed as he stood up, saliva running from his mouth. The leash clattered to the floor, and Renee pulled off the dog's head. Marshall slapped her backside.

'You needed that, didn't you?'

She got to her feet.

'Needed it?'

'I am Marshall Simmons, and I will make sure you know what kind of animal you are.'

'I'll give up the drugs, let me see her.'

'When you learn to bark.'

'I don't even know who I am anymore.'

'You know what you are.'

'An animal?'

'That's right.'

'Where are you keeping her?'

'That was a good party.'

'Is that what you call it?'

'What would you call it?'

'There is no name for this, for what you do.'

19.

6:00 p.m.

When Ronny got to Sloppy Joe's that evening Valentino was standing behind the counter in the empty bar. She made herself a martini and sat at a stool, staring out of the window, looking down the deserted road that ran through Virtue like a scar. The neat parade of houses and the quiet lives of the town grated on her.

She watched Valentino polish a glass. She imagined his hands on her skin, and she ached for him. In that moment she began to hate him.

'I want to explain,' she said.

'There's no need to.'

'But I do.'

Valentino took a Corona from the fridge, opened it, placed a slice of lime in the neck of the bottle, and swigged from it, waiting for her to speak.

'I don't normally do that, what I did the other night. I was married to a sick and violent man,' she said. 'He did things to me, things I don't want to remember. And ever since I've bedded a guy all it does is bring it back. The men around here treat you like a whore. Truckers smear the paid sex with their come and drive away. They always drive away. But you, you're different, and I wanted to remember what it feels like to be made love to.'

'I understand.'

'I'm not trying to steal you from Natasha, more to borrow a bit of your time to help me remember who I used to be.'

'And who did you use to be?'

'Somebody without these memories.'

'What happened to your husband?'

'He remarried.'

That evening Johnny bought Patty some new clothes at a store in Scarsdale. She picked out some underwear, jeans, sweatshirts, and a coat. Then they went to The Bounty and ordered food. They sat away from the bar, Patty sipping a Jack Daniels, Johnny a Budweiser. They were served by a young woman with a nose piercing who didn't say much, just took their orders and brought them over their club sandwiches.

'You said you were looking for your sister, Daisy.'

'That's right,' Patty said.

'What do you know about her last whereabouts?'

'Only that she disappeared around here.'

'Do you think she's still alive?'

'She has to be.'

'Then we better find her.'

'I think we're being watched, Johnny. I think there are a lot of men of the kind we've been running into in this area, and I think they have her.'

20.

Ronny wore her black velvet dress that night. She put on her best La Senza lingerie, caressed her body before the mirror in her bedroom, where memories slept among the ruins. She sipped from a glass of absinthe, remembering her youth and the many lovers she had growing up in Arizona. Then she walked back to the bar. All night long her hunger for Valentino had grown inside her until she couldn't stand watching him anymore, this man she considered another woman's property. She'd left halfway through the evening and gone home, where she sat drinking. But her memories forced her out of the house. When she got to Sloppy Joe's, Valentino was finishing up for the night.

She slipped behind the bar and touched his back, letting her long slim fingers linger at the top of his tight buttocks. Her heart felt swollen with desire, and she wondered what manipulations she could bring to bear on this man who was bedding a woman she always saw as her inferior in matters of the heart.

Valentino ignored her, as if her touch didn't register with him, and anger burst in her breast like a blighted rose. She watched him, aching, thinking thoughts she'd held at bay for years, as he avoided eye contact.

'I want you,' she said.

'I'm taken.'

'You don't desire me?'

'That's not the question.'

'You must get it a lot.'

'What?'

'A man like you.'

'I think I'll go to bed.'

'You know, I'm not sure I like you.'

'Then why are you doing this?'

'You think sexual pleasure simply involves doing the things we like?'

'What is it you want, Ronny?'

'To feel corrupted by desire so I don't recognise myself anymore.'

'It seems your husband marked you.'

'He did.'

'Good night.'

'I'm not the only woman who's marked around here.'

Valentino went to bed. Then the storm came in from the west. Lightning tore across the sky. Electricity hung in the air. Ronny stayed in the bar alone. She opened a bottle of vodka and drank it as she watched the sky explode, thinking about the past. Thoughts she'd hidden from for years broke like poisoned flowers in her mind, and with them came the reproaches she'd held down with booze.

She thought of Valentino upstairs. She thought of going into his darkened room and touching him in his sleep, arousing him against his will and taking from him the thing she wanted. And she thought of Natasha and realised she'd despised her for years and that her contempt was born of envy. In that moment Ronny realised that the thing she wanted from Natasha wasn't Valentino.

'Nothing like a clean conscience,' she said.

At 11:30 Ronny made a call. She went into her purse and got out her cell phone, then went and sat at the table at the far end of the bar. She scrolled through the numbers, stopping at one and hitting dial. It rang for some time, then a woman answered, her voice groggy.

'Hello?'

'Renee?'

'Yeah, who is this?'

'It's Ronny.'

There was a pause.

'What do you want?'

'To talk.'

'I got nothing to say.'

'You ever think about what happened?'

'I try not to.'

'But you can't just leave it behind.'

'You can try. My life's changed. I moved away. That's how I like it.'

'Does being Mrs. Sheen keep the memories at bay?'

'However you want to put it, Ronny. This call was a bad idea.'

'Don't hang up, you're the only person I can talk to. I'm here in Virtue in the middle of a storm, and I keep thinking about her and what happened and how we just turned a blind eye to the events of that night. What does that make us, Renee? What does that say about us as women?'

'We were in an unusual position. You know what he was like. He forced us into something. I didn't know what they had planned.'

'We could have stopped them.'

'They would have hurt us. We survived. That's all I have to say.'

'But she didn't deserve that.'

'You really care about a piece of trash like her? She was nothing better than a whore.'

'That's what men like them believe, that's why they use them. But now I wonder whether we could have done things differently.'

'It's a little late for regrets, Ronny, how many years ago was it?'

'I don't know, she was a kid.'

'Don't call me, Ronny. I don't want to remember what I used to be. I'm married now. My life's OK.'

'You still run Hot Shots?'

'Yeah, still taking photographs of the locals who want to frame a moment of happiness.'

'That's all we got ain't it? Sounds like life in Scarsdale's pretty good.'

'It ain't bad, and that's how I intend to keep it. I don't see people from my past anymore.'

'So you're nobody's mistress now?'

'Cheap shot, at least I didn't marry him. And you knew he had me.'

'Yeah, I knew. Anything to keep his hands off me.'

'So he had a few young whores on the side too. The girl's probably dead. Why worry yourself?'

'But what have we become? We're more than their victims. I still get a turn-on from dark things in bed, from things you just can't do with certain men, you understand.'

'Like I say, Ronny, I'm not that woman anymore.'

'Who are you then?'

'Someone else.'

'You've got to be finding an outlet somewhere.'

'Do I?'

'I mean, haven't you ever thought about us, the closeness of our names, like the sound of the words means something to him that lets him be the savage monster that he is, lets him do the things he does without thinking.'

'He has no morality.'

'And what morality do women like us have?'

'We're his living scars, Ronny. Get by as best you can.'

'Yeah, I still got the bottle.'

'Don't call here again.'

'You know we helped them do it. Were you turned on by that?'

'Good night.'

The line went dead, and Ronny got up from the table and walked over to the bar. She didn't see the intruder standing behind her as she set her glass down and stared at her tired face in the mirror. It was only when she gazed at the bottles on the bar that she noticed the figure in the hood and the dark coat.

'We're closed,' Ronny said, turning around. 'What the hell are you doing in here?'

'Listening to your conversation.'

'Get out of here.'

'I have something I want to show you.'

Ronny could see her black velvet dress in the bright blade of the machete as it whistled through the air towards her.

A few hours later Valentino came down for some water and found her body. Her entire torso had been lacerated, her breasts severed. Blood spattered the mirror behind the bar, the floor, and the table.

21.

2:00 a.m.

Franklin Norman got in his black Dodge. It was a moonless night as he drove to Morgan's house. He parked outside, walked up the path, and held his finger on the bell. Morgan answered, a can of Busch in his hand.

'I got some things I want you to dispose of,' Norman said.

'You gonna part me from my bush this time of night?'

'I'm talking about your buddy's possessions.'

'Who, Red?'

Norman stepped inside and closed the door.

'He's dead. Chopped up real bad.'

'You're kidding?'

'Do I look like I'm kidding?'

'Why don't you get rid of them?'

'Because I have business to attend to. Now take them to the incinerator and do it before it gets light. Or do you want me to haul in your ass over those offences?'

'There ain't no offences out here, this is the Wild West.'

'There is always a chain of command, and I'm protecting you against the law.'

'And I thought you just enjoyed the lawlessness.'

'You think it's as simple as that? Corrupt cop helps criminal.'

'Way I see it, there ain't no difference between the cops and the criminals out here.'

'You see my badge. You know what I can do.'

'Yeah, and I know what you like.'

'You work for us.'

'Hey I thought I was a trucker.'

'And all that means.'

'Well, I'm just one of your cops, ain't I?'

'Come on, give me a hand.'

They went outside, and Morgan opened his garage and waited as Norman reversed up to it. Then Norman popped the trunk, and Morgan shifted the boxes into his pickup.

'Red should never have kept so many trophies,' Morgan said.

'I don't want you to leave until you've seen them turned to ash.'

Valentino called Natasha towards 4:00 a.m.

'Someone's killed Ronny,' he said. 'They came into the bar after we'd closed and cut her up.'

'My God, what is happening here?'

'I'm standing at the end of Main Street. Can you come and get me?'

'Sure, honey, I'm on my way.'

Natasha put a coat over her nightclothes and left the house. The storm had stopped, but the roads were still wet and the air smelt of ozone. Valentino was waiting for her with his case. He looked pale as he got in the car, and Natasha reached over and touched his face.

'Honey?'

'I need a drink after what I've just seen.'

She drove home and opened a bottle of sauvignon blanc, and they sat in the kitchen drinking it.

'I called the police,' Valentino said. 'A man called Norman came by, he seemed troubled in some way, asked fewer questions than I expected and dismissed me, as if I was a nuisance who'd seen too much. He told me to leave the bar because it is now a murder scene. I didn't want to stay there. What I saw was extremely violent, someone hated her to do that to her.'

'Norman came on his own?'

'Yes.'

'He was close to Sam Roche.'

'Not close enough to know Roche wanted to frame me for Theodore's murder.'

'Let's get out of here.'

They went to bed, and Natasha took Valentino inside her hungrily. Then she closed her eyes and saw Sam Roche's face snarling at her, a chain around his neck.

22.

2:00 p.m.

Johnny did some digging into Red's background and his story about Donald Lake. Back at the Morality Inn he told Patty what he found out.

'Donald Lake is real,' he said.

'Who is he?'

'He was a prisoner at Massachusetts Correctional Institution, Cedar Junction. It's high security. He dismembered various women. The police never found their body parts. He was extremely strong and broke two police officers' jaws when they arrested him. He escaped some years ago. I remember reading about it in the papers.'

'How did he escape?'

'They were transporting him. The prison van was found by the side of the road. The officers accompanying him decapitated.'

'What's the connection to Red?'

'It was believed Donald Lake had an accomplice in some of the killings, although this was never proved, and Lake insisted throughout his trial and afterwards that he operated alone. A couple of women came forward after he was arrested and said he'd tried to abduct them. They said they'd seen another man behind the wheel of a pickup. Lake was trying to drag them to the vehicle when they got away.'

'Red was Lake's accomplice.'

'Seems likely.'

'So Lake's out there,' Patty said.

'I think he is.'

23.

6:00 p.m.

Renee Sheen was a tall blonde who wore subtle makeup and lived in a large house in Scarsdale. She'd run Hot Shots for years and had some talent as a photographer, taking portrait shots mostly, and occasionally something a little bit more revealing when wives wanted to give their husbands a gift for their private collection.

She looked nothing like the Renee Jenkins kept locked up near the railway track. Nor would she give a man like Marshall a second glance, at least not consciously. For Renee was happily married to Hank Sheen. And Renee liked something a little smoother in her man, even though she had dark thoughts. Consciously, Renee lied to herself every day. And she battled to suppress the subconscious truth of what she was. She burned with forbidden desires. She kept herself on a leash.

Hank ran a profitable furniture business, and Renee never strayed from him, at least not in a way that would have forced her to confront her own deceit. For in her marriage Renee had adopted a mode of sexual behaviour that was her husband's property, and she never shared this with another man, taking comfort from the feeling that she was shackled to a form of marital safety. But she also allowed herself certain liberties she considered irrelevant to married life.

Hank considered himself a lucky man. Renee kept herself in good shape, had a great figure, and was sexually available whenever he wanted her. But when he was away on business, she drove to hotels in nearby towns, far enough away in places she and Hank would never visit. And she did the things that allowed her to continue being Renee Sheen.

Sometimes Renee would caress a faint scar that divided the forefinger and thumb of her right hand. She would see shapes in the scar, a series of flashing images that brought with them a searing headache, and this experience always led to the need for a hotel visit. Hearing from Ronny the night before had brought troubled dreams. Now she needed to silence them.

That evening Renee stepped out of the bathroom and into a tight black skirt and blue blouse, then she left her house and drove out of Scarsdale.

She was meeting a young man called Flint. She didn't know his second name, she didn't want to. In fact, she didn't want to know anything about him at all. He'd come to her for his portrait to be taken a few days before and left her his business card. His sexual interest in her was clear. At her studio she was professional but enjoyed taking the shots of him, and she noticed his eyes linger on her cleavage as he paid. He was handsome and young and untainted by the thing that sat like a leech in Renee's heart, sucking away at her lies. Renee arranged to meet him for a drink at his hotel before he left town.

They sat and talked at the bar. Renee drank a glass of pinot grigio. Flint glanced at her legs from time to time as he sipped his whisky. Renee was thinking about what she wanted to do, getting bored with the small talk. She didn't want a conversation with him.

'So, do you live up to your name?' she said, swivelling on the stool, leaning forward.

'I'm not sure I understand.'

'I mean do you get hard, really hard?'

'You don't believe in beating around the bush.'

She put her hand on his thigh.

'Why don't we take this to your room?'

'Well, why don't we?'

Renee stood up, and Flint led the way. In the elevator she ran her hand up his leg and touched his cock, felt it stir and stiffen against her fingers.

In the bedroom they tore each other's clothes from their bodies. He looked surprised and pleased to see she wasn't wearing any underwear. He tried to kiss her but Renee turned her head away.

'Do it to me rough,' she said.

'How rough?'

'You think you've got a whore in this bedroom?'

'Like this?'

Flint got on top of her, and Renee spread her legs. He pushed deep inside her. She clawed at him and bit her lip. It began to bleed.

Then she straddled him in her stilettos, clutching the sides of his body hard with her heels, digging them in, enjoying the marks they made. She leaned forward, dripping with sweat, her expression aroused and feral.

'Don't you ever rest?' he said.

'Not until I'm done, there's a point I need to reach.'

She used him until he was exhausted. Then she did what she'd come there for. He was lying down as she went into her handbag and removed a Zippo lighter. She got on top of him and took his cock in one hand. Then she flicked the lighter on with her other hand and pressed it into his chest, running it down his skin, the smell of singed hair rising in the air.

Flint sat up and grabbed her hand.

'What the fuck do you think you're doing?'

'Having a little fun.'

'Burning me? You fucking freak.'

'Don't you ever use that word again. I've still got your cock in my hand.'

Flint pushed her off him roughly and got up from the bed.

'Get out.'

'You ever mention this to anyone, I'll say you raped me,' she said.

She dressed and left. When Hank returned the next day she was Renee Sheen again, his wife, unaware of the other woman who lived inside her, anchored to the shuttered past.

24.

Midnight.

In his Levis and needlepoint cowboy boots, his faded blue lumberjack shirt, and Red Sox baseball cap pulled down low over his eyes, Franklin Norman might have been mistaken for a trucker. He even moved differently, as if the other man who inhabited him was wandering the night. The only thing that indicated he was not part of the group of men who gathered beyond the incinerator was their deference to him in body and words.

Morgan led them through, and they stood in a dark field beneath a sullen moon whose light elongated their shadows. Some drank beer from cans, some smoked.

'You all know what we're about,' Norman said. 'You all know why you're here. It seems we're being investigated, and that will not do, not in this territory. We are the law. America began with the frontier, and it has not been eliminated. It resides in our hearts and minds, and we renew it on a daily basis. Our ways are not the concern of outsiders. You all heard about what happened to Red. I'm looking into who might have done it. There's a man named Johnny Sullivan, a journalist, who's asking questions, too many questions. We all know what needs to be done about him. Meantime, we need to exercise a certain measure of caution. We don't want evidence getting out. This place is off the map, and I want it to stay that way. We got a good thing going here. The commodities we enjoy are available to us on a daily basis. You can go about your business protected by the law. Morgan has something to say to you all.'

Morgan tilted his head back and emptied his can of beer. He wiped the froth from his mouth.

'That's right, men, this guy is bad news. When I run into him I'm going to turn him into road pizza.'

25.

2:00 a.m.

'You're a cat today,' Marshall said.

'How much longer will you do this to me?'

'I have to treat my pets just right, would you prefer it if you became a wild animal? You know what happens to them out on the highway, Renee.'

'I never was one of them. You know I wasn't working the stops.'

'But you are now.'

She rubbed the fat blue bruise on her neck.

'Are you going to get the leash?'

He shook his head.

'No, you don't wear a leash if you're a cat.'

Renee stood up and picked her clothes off the floor. She was naked and cold, and her shoulders were covered in cuts.

'You're not using the razor, are you?'

'Not tonight.'

'They've only just stopped bleeding.'

'You're obsessed by how often you bleed.'

'No I'm not.'

'That's all women like you think about. You all want babies. There'll be no babies, understand? I have ways of getting rid of them.'

'Is that what you've done to her? Please tell me, Marshall.'

'No.'

'I won't do this anymore if you don't show me she's alive.'

'Won't you?'

'I haven't seen her for weeks.'

She flinched as he put his hand inside his coat pocket.

'Here,' he said.

'What is it?'

'A picture.'

'Of her?'

'Yes.'

He let her hold it for a few seconds.

'She looks OK.'

'She is OK.'

'When can I have her back?'

'A few days, if you're good.'

'You've got to let me go.'

'No one's going to help you out here.'

He snatched the picture out of her hand.

'I can't perform for you anymore, I feel weak.'

'We can have some lunch. Then you can feed me with those tits of yours.'

'Lunch? It's the middle of the night.'

'How do you know what time it is?'

'Because it's dark outside.'

'That doesn't mean anything.'

'What is this place? Where have you taken me?'

'Somewhere they'll never find you.'

'I look out of the window sometimes, and it's deserted, no one lives here.'

'This place doesn't exist.'

'I exist.'

'No you don't. You're Renee Jenkins.'

'And who is she, your hooker?'

'She's my pet animal.'

'I need some food.'

'Entertain me.'

Marshall left the room, and Renee slumped down into the chair. She looked at the clock, the empty dial face with no hands, and she wondered when he would leave again so she could be alone. His absences were unpredictable, varying in length, and nothing seemed to have a pattern. Her wrists ached from being shackled to the bed. And she felt as though her body was fading. Even the house seemed unreal.

When Marshall came back he was holding a long piece of fur.

'This is your costume for the day,' he said.

'What is it?'

'Can't you see?'

'What kind of animal?'

'Your kind. I told you what you are today.'

'I don't know what's worse, when you leave and keep me chained up, or this.'

'What would you prefer?'

'I get hungry.'

'You're never alone for long.'

'What do you want me to do with it?' she said, standing up.

Marshall dangled it in front of her. 'Spread your legs,' he said. He ran the fur between her thighs, and handed her one end. 'Stroke pussy.'

She began to move the fur back and forth between her legs as Marshall put an ABBA record on.

Beneath the incongruous rhythm the needle scratched repeatedly at the aging vinyl. It made Renee think of a cat dragging its claws across a door, locked in a room where it had defecated and lived with the stench of its own entrapment. And as 'Alley Cat' played, Renee danced. Then Marshall put on 'Dancing Queen.'

'On the floor like a cat,' he said.

'How?'

Marshall pointed at the carpet, and Renee got to her knees.

'Ass up,' he said. 'Higher, push pussy out, show her fur.' Renee stretched. 'Now move around and use the fur.'

Renee crawled across the carpet. Then she felt his gloved finger inside her and his other hand grab her breasts.

He turned her over.

'Feed me.'

'There's no more milk left.'

'They look full to me.'

'It was for my baby.'

'Your milk belongs to me.'

'Look.'

She squeezed one of her chapped nipples.

'You better make some more. Legs up.'

Renee bent her knees.

'Higher.'

'You're ready for it now aren't you?'

'What are you going to do?'

'I'm going to feed you with cream. All cats like cream. Now open wide.'

She watched his hands fumble with his zip, and she closed her eyes.

26.

11:00 a.m.

That morning Norman got a call from Sandra Roche.

'Franklin, it's Sam. I'm worried about him,' she said. 'I haven't seen him for days.'

'Well, he's not at the station. He's due back from leave today.'

'He told me a few nights ago he had some business to take care of that might take him out of state. I've been trying his cell phone, and there's no answer.'

'How many days ago was this?'

'Four.'

'That was the last time you saw him?'

'Yes, I was going to bed, and he was getting ready to join me.'

'I don't think he's gone to the Yuma station. Do you know what kind of business?'

'He didn't say.'

'He's probably held up. I'll call you if he comes in.'

He hung up and tried Roche's cell phone, getting his voice mail.

Johnny found out more information about Donald Lake.

He and Patty were in the hotel room, and he had his laptop open on the bed. Patty stared at the images of the man she'd believed was Red's invention. Lake's face was hazy in the pictures. He had a neat haircut and features that bordered on the bland, his gaze scrutinising and amused, his mouth closed and unsmiling.

'Lake had extreme habits as a killer,' Johnny said.

'What kind of habits?'

'He wasn't a rapist in the usual sense of the word. But he did abduct and violate women, after he satisfied his hunger for what can only be described as surgery.'

'He cut them up?'

'Methodically. He was imprisoned for the abduction of two young women, both in their twenties. He took them from roadside diners, offering to give them a ride. What the police knew about him when they arrested him was only a fraction of what they eventually found out later, and I suspect what is known is still only a small part of what Lake has done.'

'What did he do to the women?'

'He held them hostage, at his house. He'd made a special room. It took the police days to find it. It wasn't obvious from the layout of the house that it existed. That was where he kept them and removed parts of their anatomy using surgical instruments he bought off the internet. He performed his own brand of sexual sadism on the women. He used their body parts to rape them, inserting bones and limbs inside them. But that wasn't all. When the police found the remains of the two women, various parts were missing. They never found out what he'd done with them.'

'What else did they find out?'

'Lake made a confession, strangely, a few weeks before he disappeared. It was strange because he'd said nothing throughout his years of incarceration. One day he asked to speak to the two officers, Scott Fletcher and Morris Palmer, who'd arrested him and run the investigation that led to his imprisonment. They visited him in prison. He told them there were many more women missing, and that he was responsible. He also said that Fletcher and Palmer had a personal interest in what he was about to tell them.'

'Mind games.'

'Wait till you hear this. When asked for names, Lake said he'd only give them two at a time, but he'd start with the most relevant ones. He added that he believed they needed these two first. He said that Kate and Sally were the two women they were looking for, and he gave a detailed description of them. As he did the officers became uncomfortable. He was describing their wives, Kate Fletcher and Sally Palmer.'

'You're telling me they went missing.'

'They did. Within days of Lake's disappearance.'

'Were they ever found?' Patty said.

'No. But Fletcher and Palmer were. It took the police in Massachusetts days to gather up all their body parts. They'd been scattered across several miles of highway.'

'How could he vanish like that?'

'I think he had help.'

'He's the maniac trucker.'

27.

2:00 p.m.

Rain was coming in out of the east as Norman met Morgan. They were standing in Morgan's garage as it began to pour down. Norman closed the door, took a slim cigar out of his pocket, stuck it between his teeth, and narrowed his schizoid eyes as he pulled a match from a Sloppy Joe's book.

'So, what's the deal with the journalist?' Morgan said.

'It's occurred to me that it's not just him we need to worry about. There's a young woman by the name of Patty who's riding around with him.'

'You want me to take them out?'

'I want you to find out how much they know.'

''Bout us?'

'About the whole deal. I want you to abduct them and do what you're good at.'

'I'll need someone with me.'

'Who do you want?'

'Burt.'

'You also need to find out who they've told.'

'Then kill 'em.'

'Then kill them.'

'I intend to have a little fun along the way.'

'Do what you want with the bitch but get the information.'

'You really think they're onto us?'

'I don't know, but the last thing I want is an investigation.'

'No, that wouldn't do, that wouldn't do at all.'

'This is our business, and we're not gonna let some outsider interfere with it.'

'I'd say we got it sewn up pretty good.'

'I'd say we have. You heard from Sam?'

'Sam Roche?'

'Well I ain't talking about Uncle Sam.'

'No, I ain't, not in a while.'

'He's not around.'

'What do you mean?'

'I'm saying he's vanished.'

'That can't be good.'

'There are all sorts of things going on I don't like.'

Norman stamped out the smouldering cigar butt on the concrete floor. Then he walked back to his car. The rain drove hard against his windshield. He stuck at thirty, his wipers on full, the highway a liquid blur beneath his tires.

28.

8:00 p.m.

The rain fell all afternoon, and thunder rolled in at around seven. Sandra Roche was trying her husband's cell phone again when she was plunged into darkness by a power failure. The lightning looked like quicksilver as it forked through the sky, sending brief flashes of light into the living room, where she was lighting a candle. She went downstairs to look for a torch in the garage. As she fumbled in its darkness she found one on top of some boxes. Sandra had spent the whole day thinking about might have happened to Sam and where he might be. And the more she thought, the more she realised how little she knew about him. She never went into the garage, it was Sam's territory.

Now she opened one of the boxes. It contained papers, mostly bank statements and old files. The need to identify a reason for her husband's disappearance was eating at her, and she began to go through the others.

After several that were full of more papers, she found one that contained an animal's head in the shape of a mask. The face looked real. Sandra held it up to the torch light. She began going into more boxes. At the bottom of a pile was a collection of photographs. She almost dropped the first one she picked up. It was a picture of a naked woman in chains. She was bleeding at the mouth, and her arms were shackled to the back of a truck. The other pictures were more disturbing. The women were all naked, some in various stages of injury, all chained up, some wearing animal heads. In one shot a woman without ears was surrounded by men with their backs to the camera. In another she could make out Sam dragging a woman across the ground by a chain. He had his face turned away from the camera, but she was sure it was him. The woman's body was torn. One of her breasts was missing.

Sandra went upstairs and poured herself a shot of Southern Comfort. She sat and thought how placid she'd been as a wife, as if some part of her had sensed Sam was hiding something from her she didn't want to know about. She'd always gone along with the way she knew he wanted things, never entering his office when he had the door closed, never going into the garage. She'd endured her children's absence, partly for their sakes, knowing how unhappy their father made them. Now she felt angry, and she wanted Sam punished. She poured another shot, then she called Norman. As she did the lights came back on, and she noticed her hands were shaking.

'Franklin, it's Sandra.'

'Still no word from Sam.'

'I found some things I think you ought to see.'

'What sort of things?'

'Pictures. Do you think Sam is in trouble?'

'You're not making a whole load of sense. What is it you've found?'

'Animal masks and photographs of naked women.'

'You mean pornography?'

'Worse than that. These women were being hurt, horribly

hurt, I think Sam's in one of the pictures.'

'I better come over.'

As Norman got into his car Johnny and Patty were leaving the Morality Inn. He drove to the local McDonald's. They went inside, and Johnny ordered two Big Macs, two Cokes, and some apple pie for Patty. The restaurant was deserted. The parking lot empty as the storm whipped through.

'I didn't realise how hungry I was,' Patty said.

'I guess we lost track of time. We've been holed up all day talking.'

'At least we reached some conclusions.'

'OK, the maniac trucker is a myth, the killings are being carried out by a group, and the rumour is being given out to protect them.'

'And what are the police doing?'

'They're part of it.'

'This whole place makes me feel like showering. Let's go back to the hotel and eat there.'

They gathered up their food and left.

Outside, a white van was parked by Johnny's Jeep. The rain was driving into their faces as Johnny pressed the key to open the doors. Patty pulled the handle and felt herself jerked off her feet. She saw Morgan come up behind Johnny and whip him across the back of the head with a blackjack. Johnny hit the ground. Burt had Patty in in a bear hug and was squeezing the air out of her lungs. His arms felt like steel.

'She can be a little fun in this ride,' Morgan said.

He lifted Johnny up and slung him in the back of the van. Burt threw Patty in after him. Then Morgan climbed inside and closed the back door. Patty heard the engine start up as

Morgan unzipped his fly.

'Well, well missy, see you got yourself some dessert, now I'm gonna get mine.'

'Go fuck yourself, you creep.'

Patty kicked at the back door as the van began to pick up speed, and Morgan moved towards her.

29.

9:00 p.m.

When Norman got there he was wearing a large black waterproof coat, his hands deep in his pockets, rain sliding off it as he dried his feet on the mat. Sandra took him upstairs.

'Drink?' she said, holding up the bottle of Southern Comfort.

'I'll pass.'

'I need one after what I just saw.'

'It ain't like you to drink, Sandra.'

'Well maybe nothing is what it seems to be, including Sam. What kind of man have I been married to?'

'It can't be that bad.'

'Can't it?'

'Sam worked on some real hard cases. He didn't bring his work home so you wouldn't have to know the kind of things he saw as a cop.'

'Is that right Franklin? Well maybe you can tell me what the pictures are doing downstairs.'

'They're probably connected to a crime he was working on, shall we go and see?'

Sandra knocked back the whisky in her glass and led him

down into the garage. The pictures lay on top of the box she'd found them in. Norman put on his leather gloves and began to look at them, holding them by the edge. Then he walked over to the mask and picked it up, placing himself between Sandra and the door.

'Police evidence?' she said. 'I saw the way you held them.'

'There is an explanation for this,' Norman said, walking towards her.

'Well what is it?'

'You know, I always liked you, you were the ideal wife, the kind I would have married if I was the marrying type.'

'What are you talking about?'

'You never asked questions.'

'What the hell is Sam doing in those pictures?'

'This'll be over real fast, hear that rain? We got a big storm outside.'

Norman seemed to be walking past Sandra, towards the back of the garage when he punched her, driving his fist hard through her body. The blow doubled her over. Then he reached into his pocket and removed some duct tape. There was a long string of saliva hanging from Sandra's open mouth as Norman began to gag her. He pulled some electrical cable from his coat and bound her arms and legs. Then he carried her upstairs and left her in the hall as he reversed his black Dodge up to the door. He lifted Sandra up, took her outside, and put her in the trunk.

He winked at her with his mantis green eye as he said, 'I've always wanted to do this to you.' Then he slammed the trunk shut and locked her in the darkness with only the sound of the rain hammering down on the black metal.

30.

9:30 p.m.

Rain lashed the building that housed the incinerator as the white van pulled up. Lightning flashed over the empty horizon, giving Morgan's and Burt's movements a strobe effect as they got out.

Morgan pulled a Luger from his coat.

'Burt, when it's over I'm gonna make her chew on this,' he said.

He held his hand to his lip, which was bleeding.

'That bitch did that to you?'

'She kicked me square in the face. I'll deal with her later, hell we both can.'

'Got some fight in her, ain't she?'

'Makes it all the more worthwhile.'

In the back of the van, Patty was sitting next to Johnny, who was blinking, trying to focus. Her face was bruised.

'All right, get out,' Morgan said.

Patty helped Johnny to his feet. His head was coated in blood.

'He needs a doctor,' she said.

'Well, hell I'll just call one, would you like a pizza while we're at it?'

'You think you can just make us disappear?'

'I know I can.'

'We got people looking for us,' she said

'I doubt it, now get out.'

He waved the gun at them, and Patty helped Johnny to his feet. He was unsteady and had to put his hand on the side of the van to reach the door. Then they scrambled down onto the mud and stood there with the rain washing off them as Burt opened up the building that housed the incinerator.

'Inside,' Morgan said, jabbing Johnny in the back with the Luger.

The building was a few hundred square feet, a cold concrete construction with cracks that ran across the ceiling like spiders' webs. The lighting was dim, and the floor area empty apart from two chairs that sat next to dark stains. There were some rusting chains with hooks on the wall and some knives on a long table that had leather straps with buckles at the side. At the end of the room was the incinerator. When Morgan closed the door they could barely hear the rain outside.

'What is all this about?' Johnny said.

'You boy, and your damned questions.'

'Do my questions do so much to you? Or do they trouble someone else?'

'What is that supposed to mean?'

'I doubt a pair like you are behind what's going on here.'

'And what do you think is going on?'

'The abduction of women from truck stops.'

'What else do you think is happening here?'

'Only what I've told you.'

'Somehow I don't believe that's the case. Who do you think's responsible for these missing women?'

'I don't know, but I suspect you do, and I think you're being used. What do you think they're going to do to you when they're finished with you?'

'You tell me everything you know and you go. We drop you off up the road and say good-bye. You don't, and this situation is about to get a whole lot uglier.'

'Why is it I don't believe you?' Patty said.

'Who asked you?' Morgan said.

'Well what am I doing here then?'

'You'll find out.'

'Shall I tie 'em up?' Burt said.

'I reckon they've given us no other choice.'

Burt went over to the table and opened a drawer. He removed a long piece of rope and approached Johnny.

'Sit down,' he said, motioning to the first chair.

'I'd prefer to stand.'

He lashed Johnny across the face with the end of the rope. Johnny bent and held his hand to his face as Burt brought his knee up and pulled Johnny's head down onto it. Patty launched herself at Burt and tore his face with her nails, cutting him below the eye. He punched her, then stuck his hand between her legs and lifted her up and threw her onto the table. He held her by the throat with one hand and ripped open her blouse with the other.

'You want it right now, bitch?'

'That's the only way you can get it on, ain't it?'

'Tie him up, I'll handle her,' Morgan said, coming over

to the table.

Morgan held Patty down, while Burt grabbed Johnny and set him down roughly on the chair, running the rope around his hands and feet and tying the knots so hard they cut off the circulation in his limbs.

'Comfortable?' he said.

Johnny smelled onions and fried food on Burt's breath as he stared into his empty, flat eyes.

'I've told you all I know. Is he so threatening he makes you do this?'

'Who are you talking about?'

'Whoever is behind this.'

Burt turned to Morgan.

'Shall we get some poontang now or after we kill him?'

'We gotta hurt him first.'

'Let her go, she's not involved in this,' Johnny said.

'Why the fuck would we do that, asshole?' Morgan said. He let go of Patty and walked over to Johnny, pointing at him. 'You're beginning to annoy me.'

Patty climbed off the table and pulled her coat around her.

'No point in that,' Burt said. 'We're gonna have all them clothes off you in a while.'

'Let her go, and I'll tell you what I know,' Johnny said.

'Tell us now and we'll think about it, meantime any bullshit and we have some fun with her.'

'I know about the maniac trucker.'

'That right?' Morgan said. 'Tie her up.'

Burt lifted Patty up, took her over to the chair, and smashed her down onto it. He coiled the rope around her and tied the knots hard. Then Morgan came over, reached inside her blouse, and undid her bra.

'Nice tits, we can have ourselves a little show while we beat up your boyfriend here.'

'Why don't you just beat yourselves off? That's all you're good for,' Patty said.

'We'll show you just how good we are.'

'Who's this trucker you're talking about?' Morgan said to Johnny.

'I believe you know him.'

'I ain't ever heard of no maniac trucker, have you, Burt?'

'I never heard such bullshit in my life.'

'You like conspiracy theories?'

'No, I like the truth,' Johnny said.

'The truth? You're in the wrong stretch of highway boy.'

'Who is it you're working for?'

'I ask the questions. Who are these missing women?'

'Prostitutes mainly.'

'And what do you think's being done to them?'

'You may be selling them. You may be killing them after you rape them. Maybe you're ferrying them across the border.'

'Across the border? Why the fuck would any Mexican want a bunch of used up American hookers? They got it going on over there, I seen their gig. They got rape houses. They got hundreds of women they use and cut up, no one cares, 'cause that's all they're good for.'

'Is it a group of you?' Johnny said.

'Did you kill Red?'

'You know I didn't.'

'Do I?'

'I had no reason to kill Red.'

'So who do you think did?'

'I don't know.'

Morgan prodded Johnny in the chest.

'I think you're the killer,' he said.

'Is that the best you can do?'

'You turn up from nowhere, and people start dying.'

'People have been dying here for years.'

'Who you working with?'

'No one.'

'How much you told her?'

'I haven't told her anything.'

'Why don't I believe you?'

'This is a setup, and you know it. Someone has told you to abduct us.'

'And who do you think that someone is?'

'I don't know.'

'That right?'

Morgan swung his fist at Johnny, catching him in the temple and knocking the chair over. He grabbed him by the coat and lifted him up and hit him in the stomach. Johnny was trying to focus on the spinning room as Morgan stepped away from him.

'Take her outside,' he said to Burt.

'I get to go first?'

'You do, but make sure you don't leave any oil stains in her snatch. I want a nice clean ride later.'

'Clean with a whore like this?'

'Fuck you,' Patty said.

'You're gonna be dripping when I'm done with you,' Burt said, running his thick hand through her hair and pressing his mouth against hers. Then he pulled back sharply and touched his mouth. 'Bitch bit me.' He slapped her across the cheek, then undid the rope.

Patty tried to claw at him again, but he grabbed her throat and lifted her off the ground. Then he carried her outside.

As Morgan walked up to Johnny, something caught his eye on the other side of the room. He went over to the incinerator and crouched. Then he lifted the object up and looked at it beneath the light. It was a small piece of torn bloodstained carpet. He put it down and returned to Johnny.

Outside Patty fought like a wild cat in the rain. Burt dragged her to the van by her hair. He opened it and threw her inside, then climbed inside and shut the door.

'Now you little bitch.'

He unzipped his fly. Patty tried to kick him in the groin, but he closed his knees on her foot and pushed her over. Then he got on top of her and began to undo her jeans. He had his hands inside her panties as she tried to bite him. Then he pulled her jeans down around her ankles. She could feel the cold floor of the van against her buttocks as she struggled. She could feel Burt's erect penis against her leg and hear the rain lashing the windscreen of the van. She was trying to push him off her with all her strength, but he was too heavy.

'Bet you like it like this, just you and your man in the back of a van, getting your hole plugged up on a wet night,' Burt said.

Patty thought Morgan was joining his fellow rapist as she saw the door open. But someone else entered the van as Burt forced Patty's legs apart. He didn't hear the stranger behind him. He was dressed in black and held an aluminium baseball bat in his hand. Patty watched as he came up behind Burt and swung it at his head. The first blow knocked Burt sideways. The second opened up his skull and sprayed the side of the van with his blood. Burt wasn't moving as Patty pulled up her jeans and got to her feet.

'They got my friend in there,' she said, pointing to the building that housed the incinerator.

'How many men are there?'

'Just one. He's got a gun.'

'Stay here.'

He went up to the door and began pounding on it.

Morgan opened it, staring out into rain as the man ducked behind the side of the building.

'That you, Burt?' Morgan said.

He raised his Luger, stepped outside and began walking towards the van. He'd only taken a few steps when the man appeared behind him with the bat raised high and brought it down on his head. Morgan crumpled to his knees. Then the man hit him again and Morgan fell into the mud.

Patty followed the figure in black into the building. He began to untie Johnny's ropes.

'This guy saved our lives,' Patty said.

'What did they have against you?' the man said.

'I was asking too many questions.'

'You don't want to do that around here.'

Johnny stood and massaged his wrists and ankles.

'Thank you for coming along when you did.'

'They won't be out for long. We need to get out of here. My car's parked next to the van, get in, the door's open. I have something to take care of here.'

He watched Johnny and Patty walk outside into the rain. Then he went over to the incinerator and picked up the piece of carpet and placed it in a plastic bag that he removed from his pocket. Then he left the building and drove them out of there. The highway was awash with rain.

Patty looked at him as he drove. He seemed an anomalous presence among the events that had occurred that night, this handsome man.

'Where can I take you?' he said.

'My Jeep's parked at the McDonald's near Purity,' Johnny said.

He drove the rest of the way in silence. Patty was shivering, and Johnny's head was still bleeding when they got there.

'I don't know how to thank you,' Johnny said.

'I know about this area, I know what goes on here. What questions did you ask that made them take you to that place?'

'I'm a journalist. I'm investigating the disappearance of a number of women.'

'And I'm looking for my sister,' Patty said.

'This area is full of abductions and abuses, and the cops won't do anything about it.'

'It seems like we're on the same side,' Johnny said. He handed him a business card.

'We should talk, there's someone I'm trying to find. You both look hurt, do you need a doctor?'

'I'll be OK,' Patty said. 'I'll take care of Johnny back at the hotel.'

They shook his hand, then Johnny and Patty got into the Jeep and he drove them back to The Morality Inn.

Back in the room Patty looked at Johnny's wound.

'You need stitches,' she said.

'What about you? Your face is cut.'

'Minor stuff. Just bruises.'

'Where am I going to find a doctor?'

'You don't need a doctor.'

Patty went into her bag and took out a sewing needle, some cotton, hydrogen peroxide, super glue, and a bandage. She cut away some of Johnny's hair and cleaned the wound. Then she poured some peroxide onto a ball of cotton wool.

'This'll hurt,' she said.

She held it to Johnny's head.

She sterilised the needle, then she ran the cotton through the super glue and began to stitch the wound.

'Where did you learn to do that?' Johnny said.

'It ain't hard, hold still.'

'When he took you outside, he didn't...?'

'Rape me? No. I'll be OK, Johnny. I just want to wash it off me, which is what I'm gonna do.'

After she tied the final stitch and cut the cotton, she placed the bandage over it.

As Patty ran a bath the man who'd saved their lives was drinking pinot grigio in a house nearby. Natasha sat opposite him at the kitchen table in a bath robe.

'It's good you got it,' she said.

'I also saved two lives,' Valentino said.

'What did you get into?'

'Two truckers had some hostages over there. One of them was about to rape a woman in a van, the other had a man tied to a chair, they were going to kill them.'

'You used the bat?'

'Good thing I took it.'

'You were expecting trouble?'

'That incinerator's used by some men around here.'

'I put the fire on.'

They went through to the living room and Valentino dropped the piece of carpet into the flames and stood there feeling the warmth spread up his legs as the material burned and turned to ash.

'You need to get out of those wet clothes,' Natasha said.

'You know, ever since I dumped the carpet I kept feeling I'd left something out, something that might get us caught. Then I saw it in my mind this morning, lying by the incinerator. It must have fallen out of the roll when I put it in.'

'I like the way you say that, it might get us caught.'

'We're in this together.'

'I killed Sam Roche.'

'He was trying to rape you.'

'So who were these truckers?'

'One of them was Morgan. I only saw his face after I hit him.'

'He was raping a woman?'

'The other one was about to. The man she was with is a journalist. He's investigating the disappearance of women in the area. I think he might be able to help me find my sister.'

'Is he called Johnny?'

'He is.'

'You've had quite an eventful night. Why don't you tell me the whole story this time?'

31.

Midnight.

Sandra didn't know how long she'd been in the dark cold basement. She heard a lock turning, then a light came on. As her eyes adjusted to the glare she could see Norman standing above her. He was smoothing a pair of black gloves over his fingers. His hair was wet, and he smelt of rain. He leaned over and cut the duct tape from her mouth.

'This won't take long,' he said.

'What are you doing to me?'

'Getting you out of the way of something that's much bigger than you. It's much bigger than me too, so there's no use fighting it. It's what Sam would have wanted. He was a good cop.'

'He was torturing naked women in those pictures.'

'A woman like you, you'll never understand.'

'Understand what?'

'The things that make this place work. Law's a complicated matter and involves many things that aren't legal.'

'You're corrupt. Sam was corrupt, too.'

'Cops have to cut corners. You play it by the book, and

the criminals win.'

'You're the criminals.'

'That ain't so. To maintain law and order you have to let crime take place, you have to know which ones to pull in and which ones to keep on the street and let them do what they need to do. Every good cop uses an informant. And that cop knows the informant may be breaking the law, he lets him do it because the information he provides is worth it. Information is currency, and that currency may mean allowing a rapist to carry on preying on women to pull in a bigger criminal.'

'You're sick in the head.'

'I always did wonder what you were like. Another man's property can be awfully tempting to a single man, especially when she's the boss's wife.'

'You and me? You're insane.'

'Sandra, there are a few things you don't know and need never know, it's better that way. But what I'm about to do is done in the name of law and order, just you remember that. I'm not a rapist. I abhor the violation of women and will serve and protect my people. But I also know that the police force has to be maintained at all costs. There is a rapist out there, a bad man, who commits bad deeds, who uses and destroys women. He not only rapes them, he dissects their bodies. I'm going to have to imitate the act of a rapist to make it seem as though you have become his victim. All in the name of law.'

'What twisted set of lies is this?'

'You can even let me do it. We can get it on, and then you will slip away.'

'Sam will kill you.'

'Sam is clearly dead.'

'How do you know? It's you, isn't it? You killed him.'

'You're wrong again.'

'Where am I?'

'In a place they'll never find you.'

The stone walls and bare floor came into focus as he moved past her. Then he cut off her ropes.

'I had to leave you alone for a while down here, while I tended to business, you look cold. Those boxes, they're gone now. Sam had quite a few of them, didn't he? I had to use my pickup to get rid of them. There's no point trying to bring down this operation, Sandra, people depend on us.'

She felt his hand part her thighs. Then she felt her dress become wet. Norman stood up and got a pair of scissors and a dirty oil-stained towel off a workbench.

'Goddamn it woman, you've pissed yourself.'

He pulled her dress down as she tried to fight him, punching him as he laughed at her. Then he cut her panties off and wiped her vagina roughly with the towel.

'So you don't shave, I like a bit of hair on a snatch, soaks up the semen. I'm gonna do his signature on you.'

'Please, please, I have children.'

'You don't say?'

'Do you think this is what Sam would have wanted?'

'I know what Sam would have wanted.'

Sandra grabbed his arms and struggled with him. She stared into his mantis green eye, which still looked human, as she pleaded for her life. But Norman's face was split, and the other eye was impossible to ignore. She sank into its liquid blackness as Norman opened his mouth and snarled the words, 'You're nothing but meat.'

He punched her in the face, breaking her nose. He tore

open her blouse and undid her bra. Sandra's eyes were watering and blood was running into her mouth as Norman unzipped his fly. She felt him push inside her. She tried biting him, but he held his face against her cheek, scratching her skin with his stubble.

'I could always tell you were a full figured woman,' he said. 'It's a darn shame I got to do this 'cause I'd like to enjoy your tits and snatch, maybe at a hotel once a week, just you and me. We could have got it on, but your mouth would have caused trouble, and right now your mouth's only good for one thing.'

'I would never have slept with you.'

'Well it's almost like you're slipping into the part of a rape victim. This is all an act, of course.'

'That's why you never married isn't it? Any woman would wise up to what a freak you are.'

He stopped moving and stood up.

'What was it you were saying?'

'That you are a freak.'

His eyes roved across her body.

'I'm a cop.'

'You're a rapist.'

'I'd like to do it again. I can tell you're aroused, but there won't be time.'

Sandra got to her feet as Norman opened a drawer. Then he walked over to her and cut her head off with a machete.

The first cut severed her neck halfway. The blade lodged in bone. Sandra fell to the floor, and Norman put his boot on her breasts and levered the machete out of her neck. He stooped and hacked until her head was separated from her body. He stood there dripping with blood, momentary peace in his schizophrenic eyes.

Then he went to the far end of the room and opened a large steel door.

'Bye baby,' he said.

32.

7:00 a.m.

The rain stopped as Johnny and Patty checked out of the Morality Inn. And Johnny kept watching his rearview mirror all the way out of Purity.

'They aren't going to let this lie, we've stumbled onto something too big,' he said.

'I ain't leaving till I've found Daisy.'

'And I'm not leaving without you.'

'Then let's find another hotel.'

He drove for miles, heading out onto the highway, passing Scarsdale and searching for towns beyond the area that was run by the truckers. He skirted Virtue and found only the road that took him back in the direction of Friskford, as he passed truck stops and filling stations.

Patty dozed in the passenger seat for much of the hour-long journey that saw a blazing sun rise in the sky. Johnny glanced at her from time to time, desire and protectiveness growing in him with each day. There was so much he didn't know about this young woman, so much he didn't understand.

She was stirring as Johnny pulled over at the side of the road and checked the map. There were no houses visible on the horizon, just the jagged ridge of some distant mountains.

'Where are we?' she said.

'Somewhere between Scarsdale and a town called Virtue.'

'What is it with the names of all these places?'

'Maybe they're making some moral statement.'

'Kind of cuts against the grain of what's happening around here, don't it?'

'It sure does. And here's another thing, the map and this area are two separate things.' Patty glanced across Johnny's shoulder. His finger traced the area. 'I've driven from here to here. The only four towns I can find are Purity, Friskford, Scarsdale, and Virtue. I've looked at different turns off the highway, but they all take me back to one of those towns.'

'It's like I said, we're trapped. We've walked off the map into a lawless place.'

'I passed a section of road back there while you were sleeping, and various turnoffs had been closed. I also caught a glimpse of another road beyond the highway, on a bend, it was closed off.'

'They've locked us in.'

'If we got in we can get out. I think they open and close the roads that lead into the area depending on their own needs, we just need to figure out when.'

'This place is like nowhere else. Ever seen any mothers with kids around here?'

'No, I haven't come to think of it. I haven't seen any kids at all.'

'Youngest I've seen here have been teenagers, and they don't act like teenagers. I think they're taken and used by freaks.'

'The area is being controlled by a group of extreme

sexual sadists.'

'Predators are usually loners ain't they?'

'Yes, but there's something else going on here. These men aren't predators in the sense Donald Lake is. They're organised. It's like they're running a business in sadism.'

'Like some kind of sexual Mafia, trading in female flesh, hooked on abductions and rape.'

'Don't you ever worry about your own safety?'

'I worry about it all the time.'

'Patty, there's so much I don't know about you.'

'What state are we in anyway?'

'Arizona.'

'Where do we find a room?'

'The only place I can think of is The Bounty.'

33.

8:00 a.m.

'Burt, get up, I'm coming over, then we're gonna find them and finish off what we started.'

Morgan put down the phone and got out of bed. He fried two steaks in a pan just long enough to brown the outsides, then he ate them rare with two slices of bread. Burt was dressed and waiting when he got there.

Morgan drove them to the Morality Inn and parked a few houses away.

'Those stitches Nat put in feel tight,' Burt said, as they sat in Morgan's pickup watching the hotel.

'He knows his stuff.'

'So what do you want to do?'

'Soon as they come out, we take them back to the incinerator and kill them.'

'What if they're out?'

'Then soon as they come back.'

'What about the guy who whacked our heads?'

'I didn't see no one, but I plan on finding out who did it.'

'How?'

'I got some electrodes in the back. I'm gonna jump-start

her snatch.'

'You serious?'

'Course I'm fucking serious. We both got stitches in our head, and that kind of puts me in a bad mood.'

They waited all day for a sighting of Johnny and Patty, and every time Morgan glanced over at Natasha's house at the end of the street he felt resentful. If he'd seen Valentino that resentment may have worsened, but he wouldn't have recognised him as the man who'd knocked him out and helped Johnny and Patty to escape.

Valentino was in the house with Natasha. They spent the whole day there. They got up late, and after breakfast Valentino answered Natasha's request from the night before.

'You wanted to know about my sister,' he said. 'I was too tired to talk about it last night, but I want you to know. I haven't kept anything from you because I don't trust you, it's because I don't want you endangered. I think my sister has been abducted. I believe she's alive.'

'Who do you think has abducted her?'

'That I don't know.'

'You think Morgan is part of this.'

'He is.'

'And he knows where your sister is?'

'I believe he's working for someone.'

'Someone worse than Sam Roche.'

'Yes. We know what some of the truckers are doing, but I think a highly dangerous man is behind their activities.'

In the burning street outside Morgan and Burt passed the time by talking about some of the more sadistic acts they'd engaged in. There was an element of boasting as each tried to better the other in their accounts, but there was also the need to talk about and relive what was to them an addiction. Their conversation was interrupted when Morgan's cell phone rang.

The call was from Norman.

'I think he's killed another one,' he said.

'Who is it this time?'

'Sam Roche.'

'You're kidding.'

'I sound like I'm kidding?'

'How do you know?'

'Sam's missing, so is his wife.'

'Well, we know he's hard to rein in.'

'We'll put it down to the maniac trucker.'

'What do you want to do?'

'He needs more women.'

34.

6:00 p.m.

Renee Sheen sometimes had thoughts she didn't want to define. They intruded on her conscious mind in the idle hours when she spent time alone with Hank. That weekend she was finding it hard to lock out the memory she held onto like a fading high of the look on Flint's face when she burned him. There was more, so much more she wanted to do to a man.

She'd witnessed things she didn't dare to recall and used booze and the separation of her mind into two parts to keep them hidden from herself, like a facet of her being she had to deny. But she sometimes wondered about the women, the ones she'd watched. She pushed away the acknowledgment of her own enjoyment of their sexual humiliation. It was them not her who got hurt, that was all, and the men who did those things to them were the ones with the problem. Yes, that was it. They'd made her like this, forcing her to watch their deeds. That was why she had to steal away from her husband and burn men in anonymous hotels in nowhere towns where her face would fade from memory like the looks she once had. But her looks had done nothing to protect her from the actions she witnessed. She'd separated herself from the actors in that drama, but they were all still reading their lines in a play that had no ending.

Renee stood in front of the long bathroom mirror and examined herself as she stepped out of the shower. Her breasts were still firm, her body full, and she was an attractive woman, but the hardness around her eyes defeated her attempts to appear truly feminine, in the way those others were, the ones those men enjoyed and hurt. She escaped by acting like a man. Had she become like them? They'd inflicted her with unnatural needs. Even the booze couldn't keep it at bay. She needed to control another person's body to feel whole. She'd enjoyed the look on the face of the young woman as they raped her that night. She had something that Renee lacked, a freedom from the need to hurt another person, and Renee hated her for that. She remembered how the young woman's face changed as they violated her. It still aroused her.

She looked at the lines around her eyes. Age was making its presence felt and the knowledge of that burned inside her, inducing a need for some greater level of cruelty, the need to inflict a savage act. Through the open door she could see Hank sleeping naked on the bed. He'd just made love to her, and she'd given him a drink, a glass of wine to which she'd added some Rohypnol. She needed to see what it felt like, after all these years, to witness it again, but it was not going to be her doing it, no it was going to be the other woman, the one who'd been the mistress of that savage man. As Hank had lumbered on top of her she thought of all her many secrets. She felt so dissatisfied. After administering his drink to him, she'd gone to wash him from her like a pollutant. Now as she finished drying herself she looked at his cock as it drooped across his thigh, and the urge grew in intensity. She walked over and squeezed it. She imagined owning it for a day and inflicting things on women as well as men, to purge herself of the memories once and for all. The idea of a woman as a rapist made her laugh, and she went back into the bathroom. They wouldn't be going out tonight to eat at the local diner in the small town that held her prisoner.

She closed the door and readied herself. She would remain naked for this, and feel the blood upon her skin the way she had that night all those years ago. The young woman's eyes had burned like a flame. Enter, she thought, enter the body of a man, for it is he who must be penetrated or they will penetrate me with their knives.

For a fleeting second Renee tried to remember her childhood to measure whether she was always like this against the idea she carried that they'd made her into a woman troubled by the need for savagery. But the idea that she was their victim had its roots in her soul. She had to do these things because of them. Those men. They owned some part of her.

She told herself things then, she enjoyed the morphine of thoughts that she alone could understand. She was making a stand against all the rapists out there, all the men bent on causing harm. Her arousal was growing in intensity as she laid her instruments out on a white cloth. The sharp objects shone against the starched lace.

One by one she set down various scalpels. She ran her finger along the edge of one, then put her finger inside herself.

'I am your husband,' she said. 'Hank, I am your husband now.'

Her voice sounded strange in the silent bathroom. A tap began to drip, sounding unnaturally loud in the confined space. It reminded her of the other night when it rained. The dripping tree outside her window was full of shadows as she sat alone in the darkness. She thought she was being watched by a figure from the past. How ridiculous, she thought, her after all these years. She no longer exists. Maybe she never existed, the way what I am about to do doesn't. That is what it reminded her of, the dripping tap. Those were the thoughts she had as she stood there naked with her scalpels and her poisoned memories, brushing the crumbs of reality away with her fantasies.

The house seemed cold, and she tried to remember if she'd locked the back door. It didn't matter. Everything could be shut after she'd done it. She could shut herself away, the way she'd done years ago on that night when a sullen moon made cruel events less real. She always felt that moonlight lost the edges that made life a little harder.

She thought of Ronny and her call. She could see her face, younger, the way she'd known her. She tried to recall if there was any shock on it that night, the night they didn't want to share. And she wondered what dark habits had attended her to ease her through the years.

Behind her the bathroom door opened slowly. She didn't see the figure enter until she heard the door click shut. She imagined it was Hank as she turned. Then her breath caught in her throat, and her voice was someone else's as she tried to reach behind her for a scalpel.

'You?' she said. 'After all these years?'

Then she watched her own body being opened up.

And it seemed to her that time had placed this distance between herself and her physical reality, a space she filled with hurtful sexual excursions because she was lost in the past. And now the clock placed her in the present again, without the distance from memory. The images came first, a reel of film as empty as all her years of detachment. But the pain followed with fast and furious intensity.

Her breasts were severed with such ferocity that one of

her nipples hit the wall like a bullet. Her abdomen was cut apart, and she fell to the cold tiles. Renee was transported back to that night many years ago when she realised that she had died, and this could not be happening now because she was no longer alive, simply a visitor in her own life who feasted on memories and heartache. Hank was not real. The small town was not real. Her body was simply a memory. When the killer left, the only parts of the bathroom that were not stained with Renee's blood were her pristine scalpels, shining like cruel stars on their white linen.

35.

8:00 p.m.

Patty was getting out of the shower at the room she and Johnny had taken at The Bounty when Johnny's cell phone rang, waking him up. Patty came into the room with a towel around her and stood drying her hair as he answered it.

'Hello? ... Valentino...'

Johnny hit loudspeaker, and Patty listed to the conversation.

'Johnny, I'm looking for my sister. She vanished in this area. How much do you know about the disappearances?'

'Women are being abducted from truck stops, many of them are prostitutes, but not all,' Johnny said. 'They're also preying on drifters.'

'Who's abducting them?'

'I think it's an organised group of truckers.'

'Do you know where they're taking them?'

'I don't.'

'The last communication I received from my sister was a photo sent from her cell phone the night she disappeared. It's of the building that houses the incinerator. The photo gives the location. I need to find out if there's somewhere they hold the women.'

'What's your sister's name?'

'Yolanda de la Cruz.'

'I'll help in any way I can. I don't know where to go with this, I suspect there's massive police cooperation in what's going on.'

'They're part of it.'

'We need to follow the players. Morgan might lead us to where your sister's being held.'

'It's a dangerous plan.'

'Do you have a gun?'

'I can get one.'

'I think we should meet. We're staying at The Bounty.'

Johnny hung up as Patty pulled off her towel and slipped into some peach pink panties and a bra.

'You were out for the count,' she said.

'Yeah, I didn't hear you get up.'

'What do you think Morgan and his buddy are doing right now?'

'Looking for us.'

36.

2:00 a.m.

When Hank Sheen stirred on the bed he felt cold and disoriented. He managed to stand up and go into the bathroom. What happened next and what he saw all seemed unreal to him. He looked for some time at a shape on the floor he didn't recognise, then he realised he was looking at Renee's head and he vomited.

He called the police and got dressed. He waited for them to arrive, sitting downstairs with a cup of coffee.

Then they invaded his home. They took pictures, cordoned off the bathroom and the bedroom, and began to ask him questions.

Norman presided over the crime scene with an eerie calm. He asked Hank about that evening and how he'd managed to sleep through his wife's murder. Hank's head felt like cotton wool, and he had trouble following the conversation and gathering his thoughts. He felt threatened by Norman, as if he was being set up.

Norman went outside at one point and walked to the end of the drive, where he called Morgan on his cell phone.

'He's killed another one,' he said. 'Renee Sheen, hacked to death in her own bathroom. He's getting hungry for the kind of action I thought we'd managed to restrain. How do you harness a man like him? Hookers aren't enough. I need to bring him back in line with business, and I don't know how to do it.'

He hung up and stared at the black sky. Then he went back into the house where his fellow officers were gathering information in what was to him a pointless exercise.

37.

6:00 p.m.

After he left the murder scene, Norman had gone home and slept until dawn then driven to the station where he filed two reports. The first detailed the murder of Sam Roche by Johnny Sullivan. The second the murder of Renee Sheen also by Johnny. Norman stated that Johnny had called him telling him he'd committed the killings and had now disappeared.

He then proceeded to put together a clear plan as to how he would shoot Johnny and make it appear as suicide by cop. At lunchtime he called Morgan.

'We got ourselves a problem. Hookers are one thing, but we can't have the local population being butchered. I'm gonna pin it on the journalist. Good you didn't pop him and his bitch the other night, because he's going to come in real useful. I want you and Burt to come along, tell Burt I'll give him a pay raise. You know the score. I hear they're staying at The Bounty. We put up a road block on the highway just outside Scarsdale. We wait till they pass by and pull them over, then I shoot him. He's resisting arrest, right? You're my witnesses. You hear him make a confession to the two murders. ... What do we do about her? She's all yours, Morgan.'

By late afternoon the road block was in place. Norman left work and drove to Morgan's house. He went through the plan with him and Burt. Then they left in separate vehicles, Norman driving to the block in his police car, Morgan driving his pickup and stopping it a few hundred feet away. Then they began the wait beneath a sky the colour of gun metal. The stretch of highway was not a busy one, and Norman didn't have to stop many cars. He pulled over a couple and told them to open their trunks. He checked a few trucks and another car. It all added to the credibility of what he was about to do.

That evening Valentino met Johnny and Patty at The Bounty. Al watched them as they sat at the far end of the bar. It was 7 p.m. when he went into the office and called Norman.

'Franklin,' he said. 'They're here, what do you want me to do? ... There's a strange guy with them, dark looking dude, he matches the description of a man Sam was asking me about in connection with the murder of Theodore. ... OK. I'll let you know when they leave. You want me to tell you what direction they're headed in? I'll do that for you if I can.'

Al hung up and went back into the bar. He polished glasses as he tried to hear what they were saying. But they kept their voices low, and Al heard nothing of any significance. Johnny was asking Valentino about what he knew of his sister's movements before she disappeared.

'You have the shot of the incinerator, but did she mention any names to you?'

'No. In the last call I received from her she sounded distressed. She mentioned she'd been waitressing.'

'How long had she been out here?'

'I'm not sure, but I hadn't seen her in many months.'

'What makes you think she's alive?' Patty said.

'An instinct.'

'OK,' Johnny said. 'I believe Morgan knows who's carrying out the abductions and where the women are taken to. We drive to the truck stop where he hangs out and wait until he turns up.'

'He knows what vehicle you drive.'

'We use yours.'

'The Chrysler's not mine, but I think we can use it. I need to make a call.'

Valentino went out into the street. It was growing dark as he told Natasha what they had planned.

'I want you back in one piece, honey,' she said.

'I'll stay in regular phone contact.'

He hung up, and then he and Johnny and Patty got into the Chrysler and headed out onto the highway, straight into Norman's trap.

As they left Al watched them from the window. He saw the car turn and leave Scarsdale, and he made the call to Norman.

'They're headed your way. That's right, all of them, including the guy I ain't never seen before. They're in a black Chrysler.'

Norman hung up and called Morgan.

'They're on their way, but we got a problem, another passenger, it could get messy. I don't mind taking out Sullivan's bitch, but I don't want witnesses. I say take them all out now, but I need you to get involved, in case they're armed. When I pull him over I want you to drive up and get into an argument with the other guy. I'll just do my job.'

The truck stop lay a mile past the road block. Valentino drove, Johnny sat in the passenger seat, Patty in the back. They saw the block and the single police car parked by the highway. Valentino slowed. He pulled the car over and kept the engine running. Norman stepped out and walked over. Valentino lowered his window, and Norman leant in.

'Can you turn off the engine and open the trunk, Sir?'

Valentino turned the key and pulled the lever.

'I'd like all of you to step out of the vehicle.'

They got out and stood by the side of the road as Norman went through the trunk. They couldn't see him as he placed Sandra Roche's bra inside.

Then he came over to them.

'What's the nature of your trip?'

'We're visiting some friends,' Valentino said.

Just then Morgan's pickup pulled up behind Norman's car, and Morgan and Burt climbed out.

'What is this about?' Johnny said.

'I'd like to see all your IDs,' Norman said.

Morgan walked up to Valentino and prodded him in the chest.

'You ran me and Burt off the road. Darn near killed us, what are you thinking of, driving like that, boy?'

'This man has been harassing my girlfriend,' Valentino said. 'He's lying. I haven't been anywhere near him.'

Then Morgan hit Valentino. He swung his fist straight at him and caught him on the mouth, knocking him to the ground. Valentino's lip was bleeding as he stood up.

'What kind of a cop are you?' he said to Norman.

'The best kind there is.'

'You just going to stand there as he attacks me?'

'What is a murder victim's bra doing in your car?'

It all happened fast. Morgan and Burt stepped towards them. Valentino pulled his Beretta from the back of his belt. He shot Morgan in the shoulder, then Johnny pulled his Glock and fired at Burt, hitting him in the chest. Patty ran over to Morgan's pickup as Norman went behind his car and, using the door as a shield, opened fire. But Valentino and Johnny had run into the shadows by the side of the highway.

Then they saw Morgan's pickup up speed off. Patty drove up the highway and turned, then she gained speed. She drove straight at Norman's car. He opened fire on her, and she swerved and turned, then disappeared from sight as Valentino and Johnny ran into some trees. They kept running as Norman went in after them.

38.

8:00 p.m.

Marshall Simmons sat in the green chair looking at Renee, who was on her hands and knees on the floor dressed only in a leather coat. Her legs were chained to the fireplace.

'Ready for the party?' Marshall said, standing up.

'These are not parties.'

'Been at it again have you? As soon as I turn my back you get some lover around.'

He pushed her in the backside with his boot, sending her sprawling against the chain.

'There aren't any men. I'm your prisoner.'

'Dance,' he said, unchaining her.

Renee got to her feet and pulled the leather coat around her.

'No more parties, Marshall.'

'You don't say?'

'I do say. I want to see my baby.'

'First you dance for me.'

'You said I could see her, what kind of a father are you?'

'Father? She's Theodore's.'

'He raped me. You passed me around like a piece of meat.'

'Because that's what you are.'

'Show me my baby, where are you keeping her?'

'She's at my house if you have to know.'

'Your house?'

'She's being looked after.'

'By who?'

'A decent woman, not a whore like you.'

'She hasn't even been christened yet.'

'Yes, she has. She's called Renee.'

'I'm going.'

'Are you? And where do you think you're going to go?'

'Out of here, away from you.'

'No you're not. You've got one more dance. You're going to be ABBA tonight.'

As Renee began to walk towards the front door she felt his hand on her shoulder, turning her, and she kicked out.

There was momentary surprise on Marshall's face as her foot connected with his leg, then he punched her. Renee staggered backwards, her hand to her mouth. When she pulled it away she looked at the blood and screamed.

Marshall dragged her into the living room.

'I'm going to make you dress up, but this time it's going to be something different and you'll keep the costume on longer and dance harder,' he said.

As he turned, Renee grabbed a lamp and smashed it across his head. Then she ran to the kitchen.

She was reaching for the knife that sat on the counter when Marshall came in behind her. His head was bleeding, and he walked towards her as she picked the weapon up.

'I'm not letting you rape me anymore.'

'Rape? Put that down before I hurt you.'

He took hold of her wrist, squeezed it until Renee loosened her grip, and took the knife away.

'Now strip you cunt.'

'Who am I, Marshall?'

'You are who I make you.'

Renee began to sob.

'In the living room,' he said.

He followed her there, and she stood beneath the light.

'Do you know who Frida Lyngstad is?'

'No.'

'You've been dancing to her voice.'

'What is it with that pop band?'

'Frida was the daughter of a Nazi. The Nazis had fuck houses throughout Germany where they mated with selected woman, just like I'm doing with you. They had them in Norway, where she came from.'

'I can imagine you dressed up like a Fascist.'

'No, you're going to dress up like a Fascist, or I'm going to sell your baby.'

'What do you want from me?'

'Play with yourself,' he said.

He sat in the chair as Renee tried to recall the rhythm of desire. Marshall followed the movement of her hand in its forgery of pleasure. Renee knew he wanted her to groan, and she barely recognised her own voice as she tried to make the sounds she used to rehearse in the bathroom before the parties, and produced an animal moan full of despair and the empty tones of degradation.

Then Marshall stood up and walked towards her. Renee carried on performing for him with an exaggerated expression.

'Like this?' she said.

'Yeah.'

'This what she did?'

'Who?'

'This woman you want me to be.'

'You think you know what this is about?'

'No.'

'ABBA's songs are secretly about the pleasure of being owned by a man, about being in chains.'

'You're insane.'

'Listen to 'Me and I,' she sings about Jekyll and Hyde. Inside every woman is a lying whore, a junky who wants to be chained up.'

Marshall put the record on.

'Now touch yourself, Renee, be a good whore and you get her back,' he said. 'And I want a drink from your tits.

'I haven't got any milk left.'

'You're enjoying that, aren't you?'

'No. You can't turn me into someone I'm not.'

'You are Renee Jenkins, my party whore, we do things together.'

Marshall poked her vagina with the end of the knife.

'I am not Renee.'

'No you're not, Yolanda.'

Marshall stabbed the woman he'd held captive. He drove

the knife into her and watched her fall to the floor of the living room. Then he went upstairs to the bathroom where he mopped the blood from his head, put on a bandage, and changed his clothes. He came down in a pair of grey trousers and white shirt, put on his coat, and left the house.

39.

8:30 p.m.

Patty drove for miles when she got away from Norman's ambush. She rammed some traffic cones and got off the road, then she lost her way, finding herself on a dirt road that led away from the highway. She kept moving, searching for something beyond the four small towns. Morgan had left a machete on the dashboard, and she put it in the glove compartment.

After some time she came across a disused railway track. She followed it and found a road and at the end of it a man peering beneath the hood of an old Ford. He waved her down.

Patty pulled over, and the man leaned into the pickup. She kept one hand on the steering wheel of the car and the other on the Colt 45 Johnny had given her that morning. She had it propped between the seat and the door and the handle felt reassuring as she touched it. The man was unshaven and had clear blue eyes that were as familiar as a bruise to her.

'Broken down, I don't suppose you got some jump cables?' he said.

'I don't guess I do,' she said.

'Could I hitch a ride from you?'

'Where you going?'

'Nearest truck stop. I can get what I need there.

'Hop in.

'Much obliged.'

He closed the hood of the Ford, locked it, wiped his hands on his grey trousers, and walked over to the passenger door of the pickup. Patty drove away, continuing along the railway track.

'I owe you one,' he said.

'I didn't catch your name.'

'Oh, Marshall. And you?'

'You can call me Patty.'

'Well, Patty, I think I have something I can reward you with for giving me a ride.'

'Really?'

'You'll see. Now turn left here and get onto the highway.'

He directed her to the stop. Patty drove in silence, occasionally glancing at him. He let his eyes wander to her thighs, and she caught him looking at her breasts as she drove. And she ignored his visual violations of her being, touching the handle of the Colt from time to time.

'It's here,' he said, pointing to a small stop she hadn't seen before.

Patty pulled over into the deserted stop. It contained a disused diner with grimy windows, two rusting gas pumps, and a truck with the letters HTI on its side.

'You hungry?' Marshall said.

'Diner looks closed to me.'

'I got something in the truck,' he said. 'Come and take a look.'

'You ain't the maniac trucker are you?'

Marshall laughed.

'Maniac trucker? That's a new one on me.'

'I could do with some food.'

'I think you'll be surprised by what I've got in that truck. I want to thank you.'

Patty switched off the engine. Marshall got out and walked over to the truck as she slipped the Colt into the back of her jeans.

She walked up behind Marshall. He opened the back of the truck, swung a leg up, climbed in, and turned a light on. There was a red sofa and a chair and some boxes inside.

'Looks like a living room,' Patty said.

'You know what's in those boxes?'

'Why don't you tell me?'

'Money. Come and take a look.'

Patty climbed in as he went over to one of them and opened the lid.

'I want to give you this for the ride,' he said, reaching inside. He turned around holding a long boning knife. 'You've given me the bone, Patty, and I'd like to thank you for that. After my frustrating evening I think you're carrying just the thing I need to ease me into my homecoming. I bet it's good and fresh, and it'll help me be the man I need to be.'

'And what thing might that be?'

'What you got between your legs, darling,' he said, pointing at her crotch with the knife.

'I ain't your darling, never was.'

'I'll tell you something funny, then we're gonna get it on,' Marshall said, advancing towards her. 'The maniac trucker's a necessary myth around these here parts.'

'That right?'

'There ain't no maniac trucker. We made it up.'

'Whose we?'

'A lot of us boys like women.'

'You like raping them.'

'What's the difference? Sex is sex.'

'You do more than that, don't you?'

'I don't know what you're talking about, but I'm done with the foreplay. I want you to take those itty-bitty jeans off, slide out of them, wiggle that cute little ass at me if you have to, pop those titties out, and spread them legs so I can get tangled up in your snatch. We can do it on the sofa, we can do it on the chair. But I need to spend something in myself before I go home.'

'And then you kill me, is that right?'

'I might let you go.'

Patty was standing on the edge of the truck as Marshall walked towards her. She pulled the Colt from her jeans and fired once, hitting him in the right leg. He dropped the knife and fell to his knees. His leg was streaming with blood as he tried to get to his feet.

'You don't remember, do you?' Patty said.

'Remember what?'

'A girl called Daisy.'

'A girl called Daisy. I'm gonna cut you open now.'

Patty shot him again, in the other leg.

'Years ago you raped me,' she said. 'I was waitressing at a diner down the highway. You owned it. You spent your come inside me, and I got pregnant. Remember now? I see the surprise in your eyes. Then you and your bitch mistress

Renee aborted it. She was so mad when she found out you'd been dipping your pecker in me.'

'That's right, Daisy, you used to have short blonde hair.'

'I used to dye it.'

'I thought there was something familiar about you when I got in the pickup. So you decided to come back and even the score?'

'I had no money. You offered me a better job. You shoved a coat hanger inside me. You killed my baby, then you and Theodore took me out to the incinerator.'

'You enjoyed it, you little whore.'

'You must have thought when I jumped out of the van I'd run home, never to return. You must have thought I'd never find this place again, this highway of rapists and killers.'

'Yeah, it was a big mistake not locking the back of that van.'

'Your biggest.'

'What do you think you're gonna do, walk out of here and drive away? I got cops in my pocket, real bad ones.'

'Like Norman.'

'Go on bitch, shoot me.'

'I ain't gonna shoot you.'

'I knew it, and when I catch up with you I'm gonna cut your fucking insides out.'

'You're never gonna catch up with me. I've got something I want to show you.'

Patty jumped out of the truck and went to the pickup. She got Morgan's machete out of the glove compartment and went back, climbing into the truck and walking over to Marshall. He was lying in a pool of blood. His trousers were stained, and he was sweating.

'What is it with Marshall?' she said. 'That ain't your name.'

'I'll call myself who the fuck I want, you little cunt. I just been seeing Renee.'

'Renee's dead.'

'She might be now. Or Yolanda is. I cut her good, the little whore. That's all a whore's good for.'

'Did you say Yolanda?'

'Get out of my fucking truck.'

'You abducted her, where is she?'

'Lying on the floor, best position for her.'

'Tell me where she is, and I'll save your life.'

'Fuck you.'

'You're never gonna fuck me nor any other woman.'

'I remember you, Daisy. You liked it inside you. You enjoyed the hanger deep in your snatch. You bled like a fucking slaughtered cow. It turned Renee on. She got sprayed with your blood. I think she had her finger inside herself when she pushed it in, and you squealed like the little cunt you are. Renee got into some strange things after that. I remember you bit her hand. She still bears the scar.'

'Renee's dead. I know because I killed her.'

'I just got done seeing her. We were having a party. Me and Renee Jenkins.'

'That was her maiden name. You used to call her your party whore.'

'She likes a party.'

'Your term for rape.'

'That's what it is.'

'You never changed did you. It runs too deep for you to stop.'

'I did change. I'm a respectable business man, happily married.'

'You might call yourself Marshall, but I knew you was Alfred the moment you leaned into the pickup.'

'Only four people know about Marshall, two of them are dead, and another one will be shortly.'

'Let me guess, Yolanda, Theodore, me, and who else?'

'You'll find out.'

'What have you done to her?'

'Why are you so interested in a Mexican whore?'

'Does Mrs. Bennett know what kind of man you are?'

'Alfred Bennett is a model husband. It's just Marshall who gets a little rowdy sometimes.'

'So you hid it from your wife. Theodore didn't, from what I heard, he kept abusing Natasha for years. She must have been relieved when he went. I found him easily, hanging out looking for hookers at a truck stop. I slashed his throat in the john. Ronny wasn't hard. I killed her at Sloppy Joe's. She was talking to Renee on the phone, reminiscing about the night you did it. She wasn't as bad as Renee, but she still watched as you aborted it. She even held my fucking head down. Then I caught up with Renee. I followed her home from Hot Shots. She was so startled when she saw me. I think she was planning to do something nasty to her old man. I saved his life. But you, you've been hard to find. I came back for Daisy.'

'You were just another fucking whore.'

'I got infected after you killed it. I was ill for a long time. I can never have children.'

'I got a baby for you over at my house if you want one.'

'You're running a slave trade.'

'My boys will catch up with you.'

'Who, the maniac trucker?'

'You ain't out of the woods, bitch. This thing's bigger than you know.'

'You tricked a nineteen-year-old waitress into meeting you at the diner after-hours so you could rape her. I thought you were offering me a job. Then you bribed me to keep my mouth shut. When Renee found out, you and Theodore used me like a urinal. I was a fucking teenager, you sick prick. You killed my baby.'

'If you're looking for justice, you've come to the wrong place. I own the police. You're lucky you ran into me when you did. If you turned up now, I wouldn't waste a dime bribing you. I'd just hand you over, and you'd be butcher's meat. You see, this is a big operation.'

'Hand me over to who?'

Alfred began to chuckle and blood frothed and bubbled out of his mouth.

'Sam and Franklin brought him out here seven years ago. He'll do things to you that'll make you wish you never came back.'

'Who, the maniac trucker?'

'What you gonna do, bitch?

'Where's Yolanda?'

'Her name is Renee. You could have saved her when you picked me up.'

'I'll show you what I'm gonna do.'

Patty walked over to him and blew both his kneecaps off. Then she raised the machete over her head and hacked into his neck. It took four blows, and she swung her body fully into them. She watched his head fall away from his shoulders, and she climbed out of the truck and got into the pickup and drove away, finding the highway that led to Scarsdale. She called Johnny's cell phone and got his voice mail.

'Johnny, I hope you're OK. I had to get out of there. Norman would have shot me, and I saw you and Valentino get away. I found something out I want you to tell Valentino. I think his sister may have been held by a man called Alfred Bennett. There's a disused railway track near the road past Virtue. There are some traffic cones a few miles from where Norman put the block up. You need to head off there, drive through them, and carry on until you find a dirt road. That'll take you to the railway track. Follow that until you come to a road. I think Yolanda's being held in a house there. I think she's hurt. There's a lot I want to tell you Johnny. I'm gonna head back to the hotel and wait.'

Patty ended the call and looked at her clothes. Her coat was stained with blood, and there was spatter on her jeans. The machete lay next to her on the passenger seat. Then she looked at the needle. She was almost out of gas, and after a few miles the engine cut out. She pulled the pickup over to the hard shoulder and got out. She looked in the back and found a sports bag with some tools in it and an oil-stained shirt.

She took off her coat and inspected her T-shirt. It was clean, and she put Morgan's shirt on over it. It reached to her knees and covered the stains on her jeans. She took her cigarettes and lighter out of her coat. She emptied the sports bag and put her coat inside it together with the machete, then she walked some way from the pickup, lit a cigarette, and put her thumb out.

There was little traffic on the highway, and Patty kept walking for some time. She was feeling thirsty and light-headed when a truck pulled over for her.

40.

Midnight.

It was immaculately clean. Even in the darkness the sides shone, as if it had just been washed. Patty walked along the side of the truck and looked up at the driver. He had one arm on the window and was staring straight ahead, a toothpick between his teeth, his lights on full beam, illuminating the long line of highway.

'Where you headed?' she said, looking up and trying to see his face.

'Going past Scarsdale, out of state, got a long ride ahead of me.'

'Scarsdale would be good. You can drop me off there.'

'Sure thing.'

He swung open the passenger door, and Patty climbed in, putting the bag between her legs. As the driver pulled onto the highway she took a look at him. His face in profile was somehow featureless, covered by a neat beard, and she couldn't see his eyes as he focused on the road. He had light brown hair cut short. He seemed too clean to be a truck driver.

She felt tired and thought of the hotel and Johnny, saw a deep hot bath and soap, saw herself naked and Johnny there, her telling him all about why she'd come back there, to this killing zone, saw him understanding and making love to her in the soft clean sheets, and she saw them leaving, going back to where they belonged, maybe together, away from this place that was off the map. She wanted to be touched again and to forget the events of that night and what had led her to commit them. And more than anything she wanted to reclaim herself from the violations.

'I'm Patty,' she said, reaching out her hand to the driver.

'Peter Built.'

His palm felt soft, and he smelt of apricots. It reminded her of playing in a field as a girl. The sun was overhead, and her heart was racing from doing cartwheels. She tried to remember where it was, but she felt drowsy and tried to concentrate on the highway, as they would be nearing Scarsdale soon.

Patty looked at her cell phone. The battery was dead. She noticed a charger lead dangling from the cigarette lighter.

'Mind if I charge my phone?' she said.

'It's bust. I been doing too many of these long runs. I never seem to get things fixed.'

'I never seen a cleaner truck.'

'I hate dirt, don't you? Soon as I see a piece of dirt I got to clean it up.'

She looked at him. His face was unreadable, his eyes set on the highway. His cabin was unlike any she'd ever seen. There were no food containers on the floor, no pictures of naked women, nothing to indicate he did anything other than drive the truck.

She thought of Valentino and his sister. And she wondered if they'd find Yolanda, if indeed she'd been held hostage by Alfred who wouldn't harm any more women. And that thought gave Patty reassurance. The man who probably controlled the abductions was dead.

She looked out of the window and realised she didn't recognise the stretch of highway they were on. She wondered when Scarsdale would be coming up. Peter Built drove on, into the night and a landscape that was hard to define. He seemed strangely familiar to Patty, and she tried to recall where she'd seen him before.

She look at his faded jeans and his black suede cowboy boots and remembered the diner where Jim screwed her the night she killed Theodore. A man was leaning on the counter talking to the waitress when Patty came out of the john. She couldn't recall his face. He'd been in the diner just before Red had picked her up.

'Seems a long way to Scarsdale,' Patty said.

'You saying you don't trust me?'

'No, I don't recognise where we are.'

'You'd be right.'

'About what?'

'Not trusting me.'

He didn't look at her as he said this. Patty reached down for the bag. She had her hand on the zip when Peter grabbed her by the throat and jammed her back into her seat. He kept a tight grip on her with his hand as he pulled the truck over to the side of the highway, then turned to her, his face inches from hers.

'There's one thing I am and one thing I'm not,' he said. 'Ever hear of the manic trucker? That's me. But I ain't Peter Built. Ever hear of Donald Lake?'

Patty was struggling as he opened the glove compartment, but he had her pressed into the back of the seat. She tried kicking, but she couldn't reach him. She remembered the hazy pictures on Johnny's laptop. Donald Lake pulled out a piece of white cloth and flipped the lid off a small bottle, tipping some of the liquid it held onto the cloth.

'You're lost, there's a whole section of road hidden from view, and I'm gonna take you there. Welcome to the savage highway, Patty.'

He pressed the cloth to her mouth, and Patty blacked out.

41.

6:00 a.m.

After Patty drove off, Norman had searched for Johnny and Valentino, but he couldn't find them. Morgan and Burt were bleeding badly, and he drove them to Nat Bloomer. Burt was in a bad condition when he got him there. Bloomer was unable to save his life, and he and Norman exchanged angry words.

'I want him out of here,' Bloomer said. 'I will not have any connection to a casualty of that nature. What the hell is going on?'

'I'll deal with it. You'll get your money, deal with Morgan.'

Bloomer removed the bullet from Morgan's shoulder and stitched him up.Norman took Morgan home, then he took Burt to the incinerator.

After the ambush Johnny and Valentino hid for some time. When they saw Norman drive off, they returned to Scarsdale in Natasha's Chrysler. There was no sign of Patty when they got there at 10:00 p.m. Valentino went back to Purity and spent the night with Natasha, while Johnny stayed at The Bounty. He tried Patty's cell phone on and off, getting only her voice mail. Al was off duty, and Johnny's presence at The Bounty went unreported. Valentino picked him up first thing. That morning they were trying to find the road Patty had described in her phone message.

They found the railway track after an hour and drove along it until they got to the road. Many of the buildings were boarded up. The houses seemed unoccupied and had a general air of neglect. Valentino parked the car, and he and Johnny got out and took a closer look. They walked up the road. Valentino noticed a house with a broken front window. He peered inside and saw blood stains on the floor.

As he was standing there a man came out of the next house carrying two suitcases. He was small, with a bald head, and wore dungarees.

'Are you looking for someone?' he said, setting the cases down.

'I am,' Valentino said.

'And who might that be?'

'My sister.'

'She have a name?'

'Yolanda de la Cruz.'

'Well, can't say I know anyone by that name. What did she look like?'

'Dark haired with sparkling green eyes.'

The man thought for a moment, looked at Johnny, then back at Valentino.

'Your sister in trouble is she?'

'Not with the law.'

The man looked at the house.

'Well, I tell you last night I heard that window breaking. I came out, and there was glass all over the garden. I could see a woman lying inside, she was dark haired, she had blood all over her. I'd say if she hadn't managed to throw a chair through the window she would have died. I never did catch her name.'

'What happened?'

'I called an ambulance, took a while getting here. They said she'd been stabbed. I didn't know the man who lived with her, but there were some strange goings on. That's all I'll say.'

'Where did they take her?'

'To hospital in Tucson.'

'Thank you.'

'Well, if it's your sister I hope she's OK. I don't know what she was doing here. This whole area's strange. No one lives out here. It's being turned into a truck stop. I only came back for the last of my things.'

42.

8:00 a.m.

As Valentino drove out of the area Johnny tried Patty's number again.

'Still getting her voice mail,' he said. 'I'm worried. I think they've got her.'

'What do we do?' Valentino said.

'Morgan's the link. I'm going to tail him and hold him up at gunpoint if I have to.'

'I want to help, but I also need to find out if Yolanda's in Tucson, especially if she's injured.'

They travelled in silence, with only the sound of the hissing highway against the backdrop of their thoughts.

When Valentino pulled up outside The Bounty, he turned to Johnny and said, 'They'll find you here, you know.'

'I'm going to pack. You go and find your sister.'

That day Valentino and Natasha left for Tucson. And Johnny checked out of The Bounty. He drove several miles out of Scarsdale and stopped at a car dealer where he traded in his Jeep for a Pontiac with blacked out windows. Then he headed straight for the truck stop Morgan used and parked by the diner.

As Valentino drove, Natasha Googled all the hospitals in Tucson and called them, asking if a young woman by the name of Yolanda de la Cruz had been admitted with a knife wound. Her early inquiries resulted in a negative. When she called the Oro Valley Hospital she was put on hold for a long time. Finally the receptionist passed her on to a doctor by the name of Grange.

'Are you a relative?' he said.

'No, but her brother's sitting beside me. Shall I put him on?'

'Yes please.'

'Hello?' Valentino said.

'Who am I speaking to?'

'Valentino de la Cruz. I'm looking for my sister. I believe she's been in danger.'

'Hold please.'

After a few minutes Dr. Grange came back on the line.

'Your sister is here.'

'How is she?'

'Recovering from a serious knife wound to the abdomen. Are you able to visit her?'

'We're coming into Tucson now.'

Oro Valley was a suburban town six miles north of Tucson in Pima County. It began to rain as Valentino and Natasha got to the hospital.

As they got out of the Chrysler, Johnny was sitting in his Pontiac at the truck stop. The weather there was overcast. He'd eaten a burger for lunch and bought some coffee as he waited for a sighting of Morgan. The stop was quiet with only a few trucks pulling in. Johnny began to feel conspicuous.

Finally, as it began to grow dark, he saw a van pull in. Morgan got out and went into the diner. He stayed in there some time and through the window Johnny could see him sitting at a table talking on his cell phone. Eventually he left and drove away. Johnny followed him out onto the highway. At a deserted section of road he pulled in front of him and jammed on his brakes, forcing Morgan to stop. Johnny got out and aimed his Glock at Morgan.

'Out of the van,' Johnny said.

'Well, if it ain't the Lone Ranger,' Morgan said, getting out, laughing.

'Hands in the air.'

'This where you pop me?'

'You heard me.'

Morgan raised one hand.

'I'm having trouble moving the other one.'

'Walk over there.'

Johnny motioned to an overgrown area at the side of the road.

'Where's your bitch and that male buffalo?'

'Do you want me to shoot you here?'

Morgan walked away from the highway, Johnny following. When they were out of sight from any passing traffic, Johnny told him to stop.

'You don't know what you're into, boy,' Morgan said.

'Then why don't you tell me?'

'I don't think so.'

'Where is she?'

'Who?'

'Patty.'

'That lot lizard? Hell I don't know, probably sucking some trucker off. She run off on you?'

Johnny fired at the ground by Morgan's feet.

'Where is she?'

'I don't fucking know. I ain't seen her since she drove off in my pickup, which I'm still looking for.'

'Tell me everything that will help me find her.'

'I don't feel inclined to.'

'Another bullet will make you feel inclined, will it?'

'You want to be arrested?'

'Arrested? There is no law out here.'

'Not for me there ain't, but it still applies to the likes of you.'

'And why is that?'

'Because you ain't part of it.'

'Part of what?'

'The set up you done walked into.'

'You better tell me what that means.'

Morgan laughed and spat into the dirt. Johnny walked up to him and pressed the nozzle of the Glock deep into his temple.

'I'll blow your head off if anything happens to her.'

'I don't know everything. I'm just a guy who likes hookers.'

Johnny slammed the butt of the pistol into his face, opening up his lips.

'Who's the maniac trucker?'

'You really want to know?'

'Or is he someone you made up to cover your own activities?'

'Hell, what does it matter if I tell you? Norman's going to kill you anyway.'

'So who is he?'

'A guy by the name of Peter Built. You should have talked to Red.'

'Why?'

'Red was a supplier.'

'Drugs?'

'Women, he supplied Peter Built with women. If he don't get enough of them he becomes a little too out of control for the management's liking.'

'What does he do to them?'

'You don't want to know.'

'Tell me,' Johnny said, jamming the Glock into Morgan's throat.

'First he fucks them. He holds them somewhere. I don't know where. He cuts them a little then he cuts them a lot. Then he begins to chop them up a bitty bit at a time. He uses medication on them. He removes pieces of them and fucks them with those pieces, before he kills them.'

'You mean he rapes them with their own body parts?'

'That sounds about right.'

'You're talking about Donald Lake.'

'You're way out of your depth, boy.'

'He came out here didn't he? You're all hiding him.'

There was a flicker in Morgan's eyes, and he looked away, past Johnny, at the empty highway.

'This ain't Arizona, this is the Wild West.'

'Why are you hiding him?'

'He serves the food chain.'

'You prey on women and hand them to him?'

'I don't.'

'Who does?'

'Speak to Norman, he's one of them.'

'One of what?'

'The men allowed to deal with him.'

'And who are the others?'

'Red, he's dead. Theodore, dead, and Alfred, run along and talk to Alfred Bennett.'

'This is about trucking.'

'Of course it's about trucking. Fucking's a sideline to what we're into, but I'm just a pussy man. I ain't a cutter.'

'Where's he holding her?'

'If he has got hold of her you don't want to see what he's done to her.'

'Where's he get the medication?'

'Nat Bloomer gives it to Norman or Alfred.'

'Who's Nat Bloomer?'

'The local doctor.'

'Get him on the phone.'

'And say what?'

'Ask him what medication he's giving out, to whom, how often, whether he knows what it's being used for. Put the call on speaker phone.'

Morgan pulled his cell phone out of his pocket and dialled Bloomer's number.

'Hey Nat? Got myself a problem.'

'Who've you pissed off now?'

'I wanted to ask you about the meds you give to Norman.'

'The answer is no if you want some.'

'I don't. I want to know what they are.'

'Why?'

'If it's morphine, I know someone who might want to buy.'

'I only deal with Norman.'

'You could make a lot of money.'

'I don't think so.'

'When was the last time Norman asked for some?'

'He just did, he called an hour ago.'

'OK?' Morgan said, hanging up.

'Where's this guy live?'

'Between Scarsdale and Purity'

Johnny pressed the muzzle of his Glock into Morgan's forehead, between his eyebrows.

'Describe it to me.'

'Small house, no upstairs, next to a garage.'

'Give me your phone.'

'Why?'

'Why do you think? Hand it over now or I'll shoot you.'

Morgan hesitated, then tossed his phone at Johnny.

Then Johnny went over to Morgan's van, reached inside, and removed his keys.

'You're never gonna find her,' Morgan said, laughing.

'If I don't, I'm coming back for you.'

Johnny got in the Pontiac and drove past Scarsdale, throwing Morgan's keys and phone out of the window on the way. He found the house, parked some distance away, saw Norman going in, and waited.

43.

8:00 p.m.

Patty was tied to a chair in a windowless room with stone walls, on which there were hooks. The room was soundless and damp. She hadn't seen Donald Lake since he put the chloroform over her mouth. Her head was pounding as the door opened.

She tried moving her hands, but they were tied tightly with wire that cut into her skin. Donald Lake entered the room dressed in a pair of faded jeans and a grey T-shirt. He came to within two feet of Patty and looked down at her. It was the same scrutinising gaze Patty had seen staring out of Johnny's laptop.

'Is this where you take them?' she said.

'Take who?'

'All the abducted women.'

'Don't tell me you think you're the only one. Women always want that, it never ceases to amaze me.'

'The highway's full of rumours and lies, one of them about you, the maniac trucker, but you ain't what they say, are you? You're worse.'

'What do they say?'

'You cut women up. You rape them.'

'I'm no different to any other man. We all have urges. The law contains that or it doesn't. In my case the system that tried to contain me failed, and I found a place where law is deemed unnecessary. There are a number of men who enjoy taking women the way they used to be taken years ago before a civilising influence that makes men less than they are came along and informed us these acts aren't acceptable, but tell me which women don't like being taken in a way that exonerates them from choice and moral responsibility.'

'You asked me a question in the truck. Have I heard of Donald Lake.'

'And?'

'I have. Red told me about him and how he bit off a woman's face.'

'That was Red, I ain't never bit a woman's face off. I study flesh. I don't eat it. We did work together, though. Red used to accompany me. He'd come along when I went out looking for prey. He used to drive the pickup. I'd let him have his pleasure with the women I found on the highway, flesh with their thumbs in the air. One woman put up a fight. She lost her cheeks. She lost more than that by the time Red finished with her.'

'I hear he got himself killed.'

'That right?'

'Yeah. I killed him. I Tasered him between the legs at his house, then I cut him to pieces.'

'He must have been careless.'

'He made a mistake, and I got my arms free.'

'You struggling with those wires? You'll just cut your own veins.'

'I killed Sam Roche as well. He was trying to rape a woman. I used Red's gun. I also used Red's machete when I hacked up Renee. Are you familiar with these names? You heard of Ronny? I killed her too. You must have known Theodore.'

'Patty, how would you like me to skewer you?'

'Do what you're gonna do and get it over with.'

'Aw, no foreplay? I bet you look good without your clothes. But I'll find out. I'll take my time with you, get your juices flowing, stare straight into your eyes as you look away and fight desire, but you can't fight desire, you know why? Because it's always there deep inside you like a burning thorn.'

'I heard you like torturing women.'

'So what else did you hear about me?'

'That you feed off the road.'

'That's true, it's a diner?'

'That you collect peoples' heads.'

'Turn around.'

Lake swivelled the chair so she could see the part of the room that was hidden from her. The stone wall had recesses cut into it from the floor to the ceiling. Inside them were skulls.

'Kind of turn you on don't it?' Lake said.

'Maybe if you're a cannibal.'

'Patty, you ready for some action?'

'I came back to this area to kill people.'

'Is that right?'

'I killed Alfred Bennett the night you picked me up. I cut him to pieces in his truck. You know him? Go check it out.'

'You just got rid of my business partner.'

'Highway Trucking?'

'In a sense. You see, Alfred had these urges, he liked to fuck women in a lawless way, then he didn't know how to get rid of them. He used to send them to me. This is the meat farm. His company transports packaged meat. It's sold across Arizona and in other states. He made a lot of money and managed to sell double produce without raising the spare, if you take my meaning. Whatever meat Alfred had from farming, he had more from his sexual enterprises.'

'And how was that?'

'Easy. He sold beef, chicken, pork, what have you. He ran a tight little hooking outfit, whores lined up at the truck stops, gave the truckers what they wanted, but the meat was already in the chain, see? The things those men ate. They developed wild urges, used to take the women out to a place by an incinerator, fuck 'em, cut 'em, leave 'em there. They were eating body parts. Soon we had a real problem on our hands. Sam Roche knew about it. He liked to get it on with the whores, chains around their necks, drag 'em through the mud, get it on real dirty with them, before he let the men hack 'em up.'

'You contaminated the food chain.'

'That's right. But Sam Roche didn't like what Alfred was doing with their body parts. Sell 'em as meat to diners? No, that was not Sam's way. What if he consumed it? Alfred got smart. Sam had a violent way about him. He'd killed a suspect while in police custody and asked for Alfred's help. He needed a respectable witness. That was the early days before the police force around here became what it is today. Alfred obliged and silenced Sam, and he and Franklin carried on protecting our investment. You see, this is business Patty, that's what you don't understand.

'The story about the manic trucker while loosely true is exotic and serves to make it impossible to determine what is going on out there on the savage highway. It is a wild place. People are getting eaten. Women equal meat. Truckers need female companionship. What started out as a prostitution racket became something much bigger. We have different kinds of predators operating out here, bit like in the ocean, bigger fish feeding on other big fish and so on down the line. The men who fuck the whores and cut 'em a little are the catfish. Then you got your barracudas and such like, they do a little more. Sam was one. Norman's one. Then you got the sharks like Theodore and Alfred. They do some bad things to the women. And me I'm the killer whale, and I'm hungry. You could say you've reached the top. Alfred was at the top, he ran Highway Trucking and made a fortune because he only bought half the meat he sold. So the truckers carried on fucking, and I got me some women to take care of.'

'Turning people into cannibals without them knowing.'

'It certainly made the locals act funny, but then we've bred a savage tribe.'

'Is that what you're gonna do, eat me?'

'Eat you? No, I live off tinned food. You can't be too careful, especially if you consider the diseases hookers carry. I'm a cutting man. I make sure they get packaged up right. There are no butchers around here who'd do the job I do.'

'What makes me think you do a little more than that?'

'My cutting is a special kind. What point is there doing a job if it brings a man no pleasure?'

'And what gives you pleasure?'

'You'll find out soon enough, Patty.'

'Why kill me? I ain't a hooker.'

'You hitch, you hook, simple as that.'

'I was looking for a ride. You think a thumb in the air means a woman wants to get laid?'

'I saw you in the diner that night. You were talking to Jim.'

'That was the night I killed Theodore.'

'They thought it was me. They should have known it wasn't. You don't have my signature. You're not a killer. You're not a real killer.'

'I'm not. The men and women I killed deserve what they got.'

'You're just a moralist with a weapon.'

'I'm unarmed.'

'You got your weapon between your legs Patty.'

'How did you escape?'

'Do you know what Sam and Franklin did before they came out here? They were prison guards. I got to know them real well. You can always tell. It's in the eyes. They already had the urge. I could see it in the way they handled prisoners.'

'You're talking about sexual sadism.'

'You can call it what you want. But I made them nervous. They allowed me certain liberties, and I introduced them to certain pleasures. We planned the escape. They brought me out here.'

'To create an area full of rapists and killers.'

'It was already populated.'

'You're saying this area's always been like this.'

'What I'm saying is things can be corrupted. There's a certain kind of hunger in a certain kind of man.'

'What you call hunger is a sickness.'

'This is business, and it's highly organised. A man like Jim is just a trucker who likes a pickle park. But surrounding the hookers are men with savage urges. A whore's lucky if she just gets cut. The kind of urges Alfred had run like an addiction in the veins. He satisfied his desires, but he also satisfied the desires of others. You see, it's about feeding people, men and women who expect their meat each day. They don't want to know where it comes from.'

'You think they want to eat human flesh?'

'I don't think they want to kill to get their meat. As I look at you I can already see which bits of you would make good cutlets.'

'So what's your technique, Donald? Do you let me keep my eyes open while you try and fuck me?'

'Your eyes will be open all the time, Patty. You will want to shut them, but you won't be able to.'

44.

8:30 p.m.

Yolanda was groggy when she opened her eyes and saw Valentino standing by her bed. She took his hand and held it for a long time, looking into his face.

'It's you. It's over,' she said.

'Yolanda, what happened to you?'

But she didn't want to speak. She began to cry and turned her head away. Valentino stayed with her all afternoon. It wasn't until the evening that she began to talk.

'I had a problem, Valentino. I got into drugs. He used me. I became pregnant. He treated me like a prostitute. He took me to a house and locked me up. He took my baby away from me. He raped me and made me do things.'

'Who did this, Yolanda?'

'He called himself Marshall Simmons, although I don't think that is his real name. He called them parties. He liked animals. He turned me into one. I thought he was going to kill me.'

'This was in the house where you smashed the window?'

'Yes. He kept me locked up. I never left. In the early days, he brought a man called Theodore to the house who raped me. Then it was only Marshall. He was nicer while I was pregnant. Then, when I gave birth, he changed. He said if I performed I would see my baby again. He took her from me after an hour. I never got the chance to name her. I'm trying to remember her face, but when I shut my eyes all I can see is the face of an animal. He came and went. Sometimes he'd leave me for a day or two. I'd get so hungry. I wondered where he went to. He had another life outside the house. He used to talk of it, his marriage. He said he was a respected businessman, but he must have lied. I used to dance for him, in chains or fur. He kept telling me I was Renee Jenkins.'

'How did he abduct you?'

'I was waitressing at a diner. I worked long hours, but I was already using drugs and I had money problems.It started in Mexico, and I tried to stop when I got to America, but I couldn't. A man came into the diner one day, real nice. Peter, he was called, looked like a cowboy in needlepoint boots. He told me he knew a man who was looking for a cleaner, that he had a big house and would pay well. He said he had a lot of children and gave me a number to call. When I spoke to Marshall he said to meet him by the old gas station. He said he'd pick me up and drive me to the house. I got a ride from another waitress. As I waited for him I got this feeling I was in danger. That's when I sent you the picture of the building behind the gas station. Then Marshall turned up. He was real charming, apologised for keeping me waiting, said his kids were looking forward to meeting me. He took me to the house.

'As I walked in I thought, this is not a big house. Then everything went black, and I woke up in chains with him inside me calling mc a whore and saying I was Renee. I'd seen prostitution going on at the diner. I took the job because

I wanted to avoid falling into that. I know many of the women have drug habits. And I ended up in something worse.'

'You're safe now, Yolanda.'

'I want to give up drugs.'

'Where did you have your baby?'

'He delivered it at the house.'

'Where do you think he went to when he left you alone?'

'I don't know, but I think it wasn't far away. More and more he came every day for a few hours. He mentioned things. He said Sonia was not a whore. He said she has my baby. He kept telling me I could see her. Then at other times he said I would be packed up when he was finished with me and I had to keep dancing if I wanted to survive but that no one would find me. He talked about a house. He said I would be taken there and disappear. He called it the grey house with the steel door. I want my baby.'

'We'll find her, Yolanda.'

She began to cry, and Valentino held her until she went to sleep.

Then he went outside where Natasha was waiting in the corridor drinking coffee.

'How's she doing, Valentino?'

'She's told me some shocking things. She's been used as a sex slave.'

'Do you know who abducted her?'

'A man named Marshall Simmons.'

'Don't mean nothing to me.'

'She said he had a friend called Theodore who raped her.'

She leant forward and shook her head.

'Shit.'

'She told me about a house. I think it's where Patty may have been taken.'

45.

9:00 p.m.

The sky looked like black granite as Johnny sat in the Pontiac, gripping the steering wheel until his knuckles hurt, waiting outside Nat Bloomer's house. And he felt as if he was about to enter a maze from which there may be no escape. From time to time he touched the handle of the Glock that sat beside him. He thought about Patty and tried to deny the images of her being tortured that raced into his mind. He looked at his cell phone. No signal.

Then the door to Bloomer's house swung open and a long line of light bled across the arid path that led to the road. Norman was gesturing to Bloomer, who sagged against the door frame, a thin reefer in his mouth, his head bowed, a look of weary resignation on his face. Norman prodded him in the chest with his forefinger and walked away, carrying a canvas bag. He got in his pickup and drove off. Johnny followed, at a distance.

Norman drove out onto the highway, past Friskford and Purity. It was all familiar until he took a series of sharp turns. Then Johnny was on an unknown road, and Norman's car began to slow. As it turned right at an intersection a fast approaching vehicle whose headlights were on full beam rammed Johnny from behind. He lost Norman's car as he swerved and was shunted into a tree. Behind him Morgan put his pickup into reverse.

He leaned out of the window and shot at Johnny's Pontiac with a Luger, shattering the rear window as Johnny edged away from the tree and put his foot down. He drove straight ahead, Morgan pursuing him. The road opened up, and Morgan tried to overtake Johnny. They were doing sixty.

Johnny edged away from Morgan. Then Morgan began shooting again. The bullets sprayed the body of the Pontiac, pounding the metal cage. Morgan was gaining on him. Johnny could see his pickup racing alongside his car in the black and shapeless landscape. Then Morgan bounced his pickup off the side of the Pontiac.

Driving blind and refusing to yield, Johnny pulled left then spun the steering wheel hard to the right and slammed his car into the pickup, knocking him away. Then he saw a broken building in the middle of nowhere, and he veered away as Morgan's pickup slammed into its wall and ignited. The only light, apart from the headlights of the Pontiac, was the fire that immolated Morgan. Johnny stared at the crumbled building in the desolate landscape and the burning vehicle and realised there was no road there. This was deserted land. He drove out of there, searching for the road again.

He drove for miles and finally saw distant lights flickering through some trees. Then he found himself on the outskirts of Scarsdale, as if all roads were circular and led to one of four places.

Johnny looked at the needle. He was almost out of gas. He pulled over to the side of the road. He checked his cell phone and got the message Valentino had left for him earlier.

'Johnny? I'm at the hospital with Yolanda. She says a man called Marshall Simmons held her hostage. He stabbed her, almost killed her. She's told me some things that might help you find Patty. Marshall mentioned a woman called Sonia. He also said he would send Yolanda to a grey house with a steel door. If Patty's still missing, I think that's where she may be.'

Johnny got out and walked to the nearest gas station. He bought a can of gas and returned to the Pontiac. He poured the gas in the tank then drove back to the station and filled up. He was feeling weak and tired, and he bought a coffee and ham sandwich. He sat in the car and ate it, sipping the coffee as he replayed Valentino's message, then he dialled his number.

'It's Johnny. How's your sister?'

'She's got a lot of recovering to do. The things she's told me make me want to kill the man who did them to her.'

'Maybe when this is all over we'll both have taken lives. It seems that's what happens when you stay too long in this place.'

'We're not killers.'

'Maybe we're still defending the frontier. Maybe the frontier is a line drawn in the sand against savagery and something worse than the wilderness.'

'It seems we're all trying to escape from a lawless place that has no heart.'

'It has a heart all right, and I'm about to try to find it tonight. I was following Norman to the place where I think Patty is being held.'

'The house Yolanda mentioned?'

'I lost him when Morgan tried to run me off the road. I rammed him. His pickup exploded when it hit a building.'

'You think you can do this on your own?'

'I'm going to have to. It's only Norman left and whoever has Patty.'

'I'll call you if I find out anything else.'

'I'm going to find Patty.'

Johnny started up the Pontiac and headed out to the road.

46.

Midnight.

Patty could hear nothing when Donald Lake left her and went to talk to Norman. What Norman said to Lake was this.

'We got a problem on our hands. A man named Johnny Sullivan is trying to find her. He's got back up in the form of some Romeo who fancies himself. You see them, take them out.'

'I'll give them my special treatment.'

'No time to lose with this one. We're being targeted. Sam's gone, so's Burt. Bodies dropping, I still don't know which ones are yours.'

'You know what my signature is. Don't mistake my work for an amateur's. And since when do you give orders around here?'

'Since I took over from Sam.'

'You boss the highway. Right man, I forgot, law and order.'

'Your sarcasm ain't gonna work here, Donald. I mean business. I'm talking about the men who poured their efforts into packaging meat. That's what this is, meat. Drifters like her, the hookers.'

'I thought you got a kick out of it, all that free pussy and a bit of bloodshed.'

'I'm a cop. I keep the highway clean. You use what you got. You take the whores, and you feed them into the machine. The end of the conveyor belt is you. You're serving the community by doing what you do. Just give her back to us in a usable form.'

'I do worry about the excess levels of oestrogen we're putting in the food chain, all that female flesh going into the packaged meat. Pretty soon we'll have a problem on our hands. I read about that happening somewhere. A chemical plant spewed oestrogen into a river, and the alligators began to lose their cocks. They all became female. We're dealing in pussy, Franklin. We're pussifying Arizona or wherever this place is.'

'I don't eat it, nor do you. Why worry?'

'I'll deal with Patty.'

'That's it, and I'll take the others out if I run into them.'

'Got the supply?'

'Remember where you could be now,' Norman said, handing him the canvas bag.

'In jail hoping I don't drop the soap in the shower? I never did scare easy. No one tried to gangbang me because I'd cut off their dick and feed it back to them in a hot dog. But I know you want me to say if it wasn't for you I'd be doing time. I'm doing it out here in a way. But of course there's still old Peter, my time on the road. Good old trucking Peter Built, who screws the waitresses in such a gentle way they all think he's a gentleman. Out here I am what I know I am and what you know me to be, the reason you hired me and got me out of jail to this place where you play sheriff. Look at the lengths Alfred has to go to satisfy his habit. Who do you screw, Franklin?'

'I stay away from soiled flesh. I like them clean.'

'You like them virginal. You're a dreamer all right, virgin land, the Old West. What you've created here with your buddy Sam is a theatre for your diseased minds.'

'America ain't clean, we've got more murderers than anywhere else, and you know why?

''Cause we don't get enough pussy?'

'Because we are by nature lawless. We don't like to be told what to do. I've created the most revolutionary police force in the country. I use crime to stop crime.'

'You can tell yourself what you want, but I know what you enjoy. I seen it in your eyes.'

'Finish her off, do what you need to do to her, and send her my way.'

'I'll have to say it was a neat trick you pulled, the way you arranged for me to escape, you and Sam. I always did think you made lousy prison guards. You belong out here.'

'What is that supposed to mean?'

'You're a criminal in a uniform.'

'I'm a cop, and don't you forget that.'

'You want to think you're better than the likes of me, but you ain't.'

Norman went outside and drove away. He dialled Morgan's cell phone and left a message on his voice mail.

'It's Franklin. Patty won't be around much longer. Lake's got her, so it's just Johnny and Valentino. And it's just you and me looking for them. Come to the station first thing, we can talk there. I've sent Reed and Samuels to the Yuma station.'

He gunned the engine of his pickup. His schizoid eyes

blazing out at the night.

As Norman drove, Lake went down into the windowless basement and opened the door to the room where Patty was being held.

'I got a surprise for you,' he said.

He walked over to a bench that sat to her right and unzipped the canvas bag. He removed a syringe, flicked it, held it to the light, and squirted some morphine into the air.

'Remind you of something? First time you got that hot rush inside you? Consider this your first date. I'll make you feel like a virgin again.'

'Fuck you,' Patty said.

But his eyes had changed and his face no longer looked like Donald Lake's as he came towards her, and Patty thought of all her dark days looking for the men who'd abused her all those years ago and she felt as though she'd fallen into night. She struggled on the chair, trying to make it topple over. But Lake held her by the throat as he pulled up her sleeve and shot her full of morphine. Then he stood back and watched her fade.

'Say good-bye to everything you know, Patty.'

Patty remembered their hands on her then and how they touched her as they violated her, forcing her down onto the soiled bed. She felt the sharp sting of the hanger inside her and her ruined fertility. She remembered the women touching her, as she was removed from herself, and that look in Renee's eyes and Ronny's hands on her face, and she fought the drug while Lake began to undress her like a doll.

She didn't feel him snip the wires from her wrists or rub the blood back into her skin, as if he were preparing her for pleasure, nor did she realise her legs were free and she could walk. She saw him lower her jeans and pull Morgan's shirt from her. Then he cut her T-shirt from her body, and she felt his hands on her breasts.

'You didn't feel the other shot, did you? They never do, first the morphine, makes you relax, then my little buddy makes you mine.'

'What have you given me?' she said, her words like bubbles, her voice sounding as if she was speaking underwater.

Lake lowered her panties, and she felt his finger inside her.

'I'm gonna take my time with you, Patty.'

He lifted her up and laid her on the bench.

'I'm gonna slide my way into your heart like a silk worm,' he said.

Patty felt drowsy and forced herself to open her eyes. She was staring at the skulls in the wall. She saw Lake's face swim into view. He was holding something in his hand.

As she looked at it, the object held no reference or meaning for her, as if it was unknown and lay outside her experience. It was imbued only with a sense of obscenity. Then she realised what it was and she recoiled. Lake was holding a bone, long and clean with a joint at the end like the head of a phallus.

'I pulled this out of one young woman who was particularly dirty. She'd give it up for any trucker who came along. She used to dance, naked, swaying her ass at you, touching herself, selling her flesh. Well her flesh is still for sale, but not in the way she meant it to be. I guess you could say her dancing days are over, now she's giving something to you.'

Lake lowered the bone. Then Patty began to scream in the stone room.

47.

2:00 a.m.

Johnny found the road where he lost Norman. He took a right turn where Norman had, then he drove for miles, seeing no houses. The landscape was barren, the area was uninhabited. It lay beyond the blocked off highway he'd seen the day he and Patty left the Morality Inn.

He drove for hours, covering every part of the terrain. The road looped around on itself, forcing him to return to where he'd started and he began again, checking how many miles it took for him to get to the point where he seemed to have no choice but to follow the curve back. He stopped and got out there. He looked around, seeing only the road that bore him back. Then he noticed some logs stacked up by the side of the road. Johnny walked over and saw a path behind them, large enough to get a vehicle through. He moved them out of the way and saw tire tracks. He followed the path and came out onto another road.

After several miles he came to a fork. The left one led back to where he came from. He took the right one. He mounted a hill. On the other side was a building. Johnny parked and got out. He removed a torch from the glove compartment and put the Glock in the back of his belt.

His torch showed him a grey building with a steel door at the front. He took a shot of it. He checked his phone for a signal. It showed one bar. He sent the shot to Valentino. He also sent a text to him that read, 'The road past Scarsdale off the highway runs for miles. When you see a right turn, take it. There's a path. I've removed the logs from it. Go through it and over the hill, then bear right and you'll find it. If you don't hear from me this is where I am. I'm going in for Patty.'

Johnny put his phone in his pocket and drew his Glock. He walked around the building looking for a way in. At the rear he found a window. He smashed it with the butt of his gun, knocked the shards of glass away from it, and climbed inside. He was standing in a kitchen. Cans of food covered an entire wall, stacked neatly one on top of the other. A meat cleaver lay lodged in a large block of wood.

Johnny listened for movement. The house was silent. He tried the handle of the door and went out into a corridor. An incongruously neat living room was to the right. The light was on, and Johnny went inside. There was a sofa, a chair, bare floor boards, and a gold fish bowl full of sand. A shell of a TV set on a table.

Across the corridor was a bedroom. It contained a single bed with dark blue satin sheets and a clock that bore the letters HTI on it. Someone had drawn a naked woman on the face in black felt tip. She had a heavily made up mouth, and her body faded at the edge of the clock. The glass had been removed and the hands pulled outwards so that it looked as though the woman was clapping. The words, 'No time like meat time' had been written on the face.

The next room contained more cans of food. A machete sat on a chair. Johnny left and tried the next door which led into the bathroom. A spotless white bath and a toilet. A sink with a dripping tap. A bathroom cabinet full of empty pill bottles and razor blades. An empty trash can. A plastic shower curtain. Extremely clean.

Johnny went back into the corridor. There was another door at the end. He opened it slowly, his Glock raised, and he saw steps. Then he went down into the basement.

Johnny stood by the door at the bottom listening for a sound. Complete silence. He turned the handle slowly. He could see stone walls and a table. He inched forward, holding his Glock in front of him as more of the room came into view. He could make out the edge of the bench and a chair, as he walked in. Then Donald Lake smashed him across the arm with an iron bar, knocking the gun out of his hand. Lake pressed the muzzle of a snub-nosed revolver against Johnny's temple.

'Come in, you can be part of the action,' Lake said. 'This is an old sheriff's model. Fitting, I'd say, since you've stumbled into the most lawless place in the United States.'

Johnny could see Patty behind the door. She was gagged and naked, and he looked away. Lake pushed him over to a chair. Then he motioned with the gun.

'Sit down. I'm gonna tie you up and make you watch the fun and games I got planned for her. That's why you came, ain't it, to see the peep show?'

As Lake tied him to the chair, Johnny tried to make eye contact with Patty, who was shackled to a hook on a wall.

'Now, I was about to do a little cutting when you came along, so you can watch. Then you can feed all the hungry diners. We got a good business proposition, one that satisfies the locals and makes a lot of money. You'll never be found.'

'You're packaging human flesh.'

'I am, Johnny. I take that to be your name. This is the end

of the road, a small dank cellar with me in it, just me and my good old knives. Slice by slice, I prepare the next shipment that will travel the savage highway.'

'What will you do when you run out of bodies?'

'I'll never run out of bodies, there's a plentiful supply. My bowl is full of sand. There is no time for me. My hourglass will never run down.'

'That why you got the gold fish bowl up there?'

'I like symbolic things, like broken bones placed inside a bleached jaw and set upon an axle covered in grease. I've been doing this for years. I swim in time like a shark in a pool of bleeding fish.'

'You're crazy. What will you do if Norman turns you in?'

'Norman won't ever turn me in.'

'You don't think if the law catches up with him he won't use his position as a cop to make sure they know who you are and where you came from?'

'Do you know where you are? We're not even in the same century as anyone else.'

'Whatever you say, this is the United States.'

'You chose the highway, Johnny, now you gotta pay, but first I'm going to make you part of it.'

Lake kicked the door shut. He turned Johnny around so he was facing Patty. Johnny saw the skulls embedded in the stone wall and stared at his Glock lying on the floor over by the door. Then Lake picked a knife up from the table.

'Johnny, this is a boning knife. I use it on whores of all kinds. I use it to maintain the highway around here and supply the diners with the meat they need. We all need meat of one kind or another.'

Johnny struggled with the wires on his wrists as Lake

walked over to Patty and placed the tip of the knife between her legs.

'Sing for me, Patty.'

Patty pulled back, pressing her buttocks against the wall.

'Animals,' Lake said.

He moved away from her and walked over to the far end of the room. He took hold of one of the hooks in the wall and turned it, opening a section of wall. Johnny could smell something feral. Then a large grey wolf entered the stone room.

'The truckers wear masks when they kill. Sam Roche used to go on the prowl wearing a wolf's head, but I am more lupine than anything you'll ever meet. I'll put you all in chains,' Lake said.

The wolf walked over to Patty and stuck his nose between her legs.

'I was raised by wolves,' Lake said. 'Now give him what he wants, Patty, he's hungry.'

Johnny struggled to free himself as the wolf snarled, and Lake tore the duct tape from Patty's mouth.

'You're going to feed the beast,' he said. 'Then you're going to feed the diners.'

Lake began to howl as the door opened behind him and Valentino entered the room.

Then Valentino shot Lake twice with his Beretta. The noise startled the wolf, and it ran out through the door and up the stairs into the building. Valentino stood over Lake and emptied the gun into his head.

'Is there anyone else in the house?' Valentino said.

'No, just him, I checked it when I came in,' Johnny said.

Valentino cut the wires from Patty's arms and legs with

some pliers he found lying on the table.

'Are you hurt?' he said.

'He raped me with a bone. My thigh's cut, but he didn't reach the rest of me with the knife.'

Valentino was wearing a long coat. He took it off and put it on Patty. Then he untied Johnny and handed him his Glock.

Lake's face looked like butchered meat, and he lay staring at the ceiling with animal eyes as they left the building and headed out into the night.

48.

7:00 a.m.

It was almost five o'clock when Valentino rescued them. He'd become concerned after speaking to Johnny and left Natasha at the hospital with Yolanda. He drove to Scarsdale and got Johnny's two texts. He found the building and got in the same way Johnny had.

After he shot Lake, Valentino followed Johnny as he drove Patty out of there. Johnny found the highway and stopped. Valentino got out of the Chrysler and walked over to them.

'I think he broke my arm,' Johnny said.

'Come to the hospital in Tucson with me.'

'I don't think I can drive much further.'

'I'll drive.'

Johnny pulled the Pontiac further off the highway, and they got in the Chrysler. He took a bag out of the trunk and handed it to Patty.

'I brought your clothes from The Bounty,' he said.

Johnny and Valentino waited in the Chrysler while Patty changed in the Pontiac. She came out in jeans, sneakers, a T-shirt, and denim jacket and gave Valentino his coat back.

Johnny locked the Pontiac, and he and Patty got in the back of the Chrysler. Then Valentino drove on, back onto the highway, into the morning light.

Johnny reached over with his good arm and laid his hand on Valentino's shoulder.

'That's the second time you've saved our lives.'

'After what Yolanda told me, I had to find Patty. I had to do it for all the women these men have harmed and killed.'

'You found your sister?' Patty said. 'How is she?'

'She's recovering.'

Valentino drove on, past Scarsdale.

'You know, you mentioned a man named Marshall. You also said he talked about Sonia to your sister,' Johnny said. 'Alfred Bennett's wife is called Sonia.'

'From what Yolanda has said, this man Marshall was leading a double life.'

'Alfred Bennett has to be behind this. He owns Highway Trucking. If that's the case he'll come after us. How many of them are there left?'

'He's dead,' Patty said.

Johnny turned around and looked at her.

'How do you know?'

'There are some things I want to tell you.'

While Alfred Bennett was dead, Norman was still very much alive. Just then he rammed Valentino off the road in his pickup.

49.

7:45 a.m.

Valentino was nudged against the hard shoulder. Norman pushed him until the Chrysler came up against a bank and couldn't move. Then he got out of his pickup and aimed a Winchester rifle at the windshield. Valentino tried reversing, but his tires just spun.

'Throw out your weapons and get out of the car,' Norman said. 'Or I'll begin shooting.'

Valentino glanced at Johnny.

'I think we have no other option,' he said.

He opened his window and slung his Beretta across the hood of the Chrysler. Johnny tossed his Glock out.

'What about the bitch?' Norman said.

'She's unarmed,' Johnny said, through the open window.

They got out with their hands raised. Norman dragged Patty over to the pickup and frisked her, keeping the Winchester trained on Johnny and Valentino.

'It's over,' Johnny said. 'Donald Lake's dead, so's Morgan. What have you got left?'

'What have I got left? This is a huge business. Do you have any idea how much money's involved in it? You don't just shut it down. I'm going to kill you all. It's suitable this gun won the West, because that's what I got left.'

'So get it over and done with,' Patty said.

'Not here, I got to dispose of you.'

Norman reached into the back of his pickup and slung a rope at Valentino.

'Tie their arms and make it tight.'

Valentino walked over to Johnny, then turned to Norman.

'He's got a broken arm.'

'Tough shit.'

'Sorry,' Valentino said to Johnny.

He tied Johnny's arms behind his back and heard him wince.

'I figured something had happened to Morgan. Which one of you killed him?' Norman said.

'I ran him off the road,' Johnny said. 'His pickup caught fire.'

'That right? Then I'm gonna leave you till last.'

Norman tossed another rope over to Valentino.

'That's for the bitch.'

Valentino tied Patty's wrists behind her back.

'Now put them in the back of the pickup,' Norman said.

Valentino lifted Patty on, then helped Johnny up. Then Norman slammed the butt of his rifle into the back of Valentino's head. He tied him up and lifted him over his shoulder, throwing him into the back of the pickup like a sack of coal.

He got in and started the engine, accelerating rapidly so they were jostled in the back. Norman took them on the highway back past Scarsdale, all the way to the incinerator.

50.

9:00 a.m.

Valentino came to as they got there. His head was bleeding, and his hands felt numb from the rope. Johnny was in pain and sweating. Norman got out and came over to them, his rifle aimed at Valentino, as he lowered the tailgate.

'Get out,' he said.

Valentino got to his feet and helped Patty down, then he jumped out and lifted a hand to Johnny, who clambered out. They stood in a line with Norman before them, his back to the incinerator and the field behind it. It was an overcast morning, and rain clouds gathered on the horizon.

'You've cost me a lot of money. I ain't gonna let a group of strangers come here and do that. Alfred and Theodore funded the police force. Highway Trucking will continue. I'm the new owner. First I'm gonna finish what Morgan should have done the other night.'

'I've already written the story about your operation,' Johnny said. 'It runs tomorrow. You'll have every news station crawling all over you.'

'I don't think so.'

'Ain't you gonna try to screw me like your buddies did?' Patty said.

'I lost my appetite.'

'You mean you're not gonna get your kicks?'

'There are plenty more whores out there. The stops will be buzzing with hookers tonight, and I want this over and done with.'

'So what are you going to do?' Johnny said.

'I'm going to kill them both, make you watch, torture you to death, then get rid of you.'

'You know things are over for you, don't you?' Valentino said.

'How do you figure that?'

'Do you think you know everything that happens in this area?'

'I own this area.'

'There's always the unexpected.'

Norman began to laugh, his green and black eyes deranged. As Patty looked at him she remembered Sam Roche wearing the wolf's head the night she shot him.

'Get inside,' Norman said.

He pointed at the incinerator.

He was still laughing as Natasha fired two rounds from a Remington 700 into the back of his head. She took the top of his skull off.

Norman fell face forward. Natasha fired two more rounds into his head, splitting it apart and spraying the earth with blood and bone. Then she walked over to Valentino, kissed him on the mouth, and untied him.

51.

9:30 a.m.

As Natasha untied Johnny and Patty, Valentino rolled Norman over. He had no face left, but his eyes were open and they stared out of his wasted flesh. They got into the Chrysler 200 that Natasha had driven there in. She drove out onto the highway.

'How did you find us?' Valentino said.

'I left soon after you. I knew you were in danger. I hired this car and drove home, got the Remington, then went straight to Scarsdale. I figured you were looking for Johnny there. I saw Norman holding you up on the highway. You were getting in the back of his pickup, and I tailed you.'

'We were heading to the hospital when he ambushed us. Johnny's got a broken arm, and I think Patty should see a doctor.'

'I'll get us there as soon as I can, and your head's bleeding, honey.'

'How's Yolanda?' Valentino said.

'She was sleeping when I left her. I wrote a note saying I'd be back in a few hours.'

'I think we should get her baby before we leave the area.'

'Where is her baby?' Johnny said.

'From what Yolanda told me, this man Marshall or Alfred took her away as soon as she was born. She thinks she's with his wife, Sonia.'

'I met Alfred. I asked him about the missing women. Let's go there now, I remember the address.'

'I know where she lives,' Natasha said.

'Are we expecting trouble?' Valentino said.

'I don't know Sonia well, but I don't think she's part of the corruption.'

Valentino applied some gauze from the first aid kit to his head, sticking it down with bandages as Natasha drove. They entered Virtue and passed Sloppy Joe's. The windows were boarded up and a For Sale sign stood outside.

Natasha parked, and they got out of the Chrysler and walked to the house. It all looked pristine, with the well-tended lawn, the flag on the pole, the polished windows, and immaculate paintwork.

Valentino rang the bell.

After some time Sonia answered. She wore a pair of faded designer jeans and a pale blue blouse. There was a film of perspiration on her forehead.

'Yes, how can I help you?' she said.

She glanced at everyone and paused at Natasha.

'It's about your husband,' Johnny said.

'I know you. You're a journalist.'

'That's right.'

'He's away on business.'

'Can we come inside?'

'I don't know what you want.'

'It will be much easier if we talk inside,' Natasha said.

Sonia stepped back, and they walked into the hallway.

'Does the name Marshall Simmons mean anything to you?' Valentino said as he closed the door.

'No.'

'Do you know what sort of business your husband is away on?'

'Look, who are you?'

'My name is Valentino. This is Natasha and Patty. You know Johnny.'

'I haven't seen you in years,' she said to Natasha. 'I heard about Theodore.'

'Yeah, well, marriage to him kind of ruined my social life.'

'Can you tell me what this is about?'

'I don't know if you're aware of how Theodore treated me.'

'I heard you were having problems.'

'Has it ever occurred to you why he used to visit Alfred on his own?'

'They talked business together. I was rarely involved.'

'Theodore didn't want me talking to people.'

'About what?'

'How he got his kicks.'

'Look, what has this got to do with Alfred?'

'You have something that belongs to us,' Valentino said.

Just then a baby's cry broke through the conversation.

'I have to go,' Sonia said.

The sound was coming from upstairs, and Valentino

started up the staircase.

'What do you think you're doing?' Sonia said, going after him.

Johnny, Natasha, and Patty followed. As Valentino reached the first floor Sonia grabbed his arm.

'You stay away from my daughter.'

'She's not your daughter, is she?'

'How dare you speak to me like that?'

She slapped him across the cheek.

'She's my sister's daughter.'

'What are you talking about?'

'Sonia,' Natasha said. 'Alfred and Theodore were running a prostitution ring. Alfred was leading a double life under the name Marshall Simmons. He abducted Valentino's sister and raped her. You didn't give birth to this baby.'

'She's adopted.'

'Do you have the papers?' Johnny said.

'What?'

'Do you have the adoption papers?'

She flushed.

'Alfred has.'

'I don't believe you,' Valentino said. 'We can get DNA tests.'

'This is outrageous. You have no right coming here like this.'

The baby began to cry again. The sound was louder, more insistent, and Valentino opened the second door on the right. It was a white room, and the shades were drawn. Lying in a cot was a dark-eyed baby, and he lifted her out.

'Put her down,' Sonia said.

The others had all come into the room.

Sonia marched towards Valentino as his cell phone began to ring. He handed the baby to Natasha and answered it.

'Yes, Yolanda, we're OK. How are you feeling? ... We're coming back with your daughter. ... That's right. There's someone I think you should speak to, Sonia's been looking after her. Yes, she's fine. She looks beautiful, can you hear her cry?'

He held out the phone to Sonia, who took a step back.

'Talk to my sister, what have you got to fear if there's nothing wrong here?'

Sonia took the phone from him.

'Hello?'

Valentino took his niece in his arms, and she stopped crying. The conversation Sonia had with Yolanda was audible in the room.

'Is my baby all right?' Yolanda said.

'I don't know why you think she's yours.'

'Were you married to Marshall?'

'I'm married to Alfred.'

'You need to give her to me.'

'I don't have to do anything.'

'Are you looking after her?'

'Yes.'

'I'll tell you something only her mother could know. If she is my baby, then she has a birthmark on the inside of her right thigh. Have you seen it?'

Sonia handed the phone to Natasha and left the room.

'Yolanda, we're bringing her back,' Natasha said.

They found Sonia sitting downstairs in the kitchen with a glass of water in her hand and a box of pills in front of her on the table.

'How did she know that?' she said. 'No one's seen her, apart from Alfred and me.'

'Sonia, I think you're an innocent party,' Johnny said. 'I think your husband lied to you throughout your marriage. I think he effectively hid who he was from you, and I think you know when he brought you that baby it was illegal.'

'Who did he adopt it from?' Natasha said.

'We couldn't have children. We couldn't adopt, either.'

'Why?' Natasha said.

'Because I have a mental history.'

'Where did Alfred say he got the baby from?'

'Mexico. He said he bought it from a family down there. I wanted a child so much. I'm not mad. I had some problems when I was younger. I'm not schizophrenic. It was all hormonal.'

'Did Alfred want children?' Natasha said.

'He said watching a mother breastfeed was one of the most beautiful sights in the world.'

'Alfred and Theodore raped me and killed my baby. Did you know his ex-wife and mistress?' Patty said.

'He was a good man.'

'How did he hide it from you?'

'Hide what? He didn't want to see Ronny after he divorced, and I respected that. Alfred worked hard and was a good husband to me. He had a terrible childhood. His mother never showed him any affection. She was British. Alfred was torn about his nationality, saying he was an American through and through. His mother never breastfed him. Then she had another boy. Alfred was a private man, he never used to talk much about the past, but he did tell me once that he used to watch his mother feed his brother and he felt tremendous jealousy and rage.'

'Sonia, I remember in the early days of your marriage, you were having problems with Alfred,' Natasha said. 'You remember? You told me about him wanting you to dress up.'

'It was in the early weeks.'

'You found Nazi uniforms in a wardrobe.'

'It stopped. I threatened to leave him.'

'How do you think he stopped?' Natasha said.

Sonia turned her gaze to the baby in Valentino's arms.

'She's a beautiful child, but he stole her.'

'And she belongs with her mother,' Valentino said.

Sonia stood up.

'Can I say good-bye to her?'

'Of course.'

Valentino handed her the baby.

Sonia bent her head, and they could see tears gathering in her eyes.

'I did look after you. You're a beautiful child. Do try to remember the time we had together, Renee.'

She handed her to Valentino.

'Renee?' he said.

'Alfred named her. I never thought it suited her.'

They left the house and got in the Chrysler. Valentino sat in the back with the baby.

'Did you notice the medication she was taking?' Johnny

said. 'It's what they give to schizophrenics.'

'All Alfred gave her was stolen things, including who he pretended to be,' Patty said.

They were silent as they left Virtue.

As Natasha drove she passed the stretch of highway where Johnny's Pontiac was parked.

'My car's over there,' he said.

'I'll drive you, and Patty can stay with Natasha,' Valentino said. 'The baby can sleep on the passenger seat.'

52.

7:00 p.m.

They stopped for sandwiches on the way to Tucson. When they got to the hospital Johnny went to get his arm looked at and Patty was examined by a female doctor. She said she'd been attacked by an unknown assailant. Valentino got his head stitched. Johnny and Patty found him and Natasha in Yolanda's room that evening.

They sat on chairs by her bed. Yolanda looked pale, but already some of the stress and pain on her face was fading. Her baby was sleeping in her arms.

'The man who held you prisoner was called Alfred Bennett,' Patty said.

'He kept telling me I was Renee. He called himself Marshall. I think he was a split personality.'

'You don't need to worry about him anymore. He's dead,' Patty said.

She noticed Johnny's gaze linger on her.

'Patty was the one who helped us find you,' Valentino said.

'Well, thank you.' Yolanda put her hand on Patty's. 'I hear you've been through an ordeal too.'

'I guess we all have some putting behind us to do,' Natasha said.

'We're planning to leave in a few days when Yolanda is able to travel,' Valentino said. 'In the meantime we're going to stay at a hotel nearby. Then we return to Purity and pack up our things. Natasha has sold her house.'

'I've also got an offer on the café.'

'You both saved our lives,' Johnny said, standing up. 'I won't forget you. You know how to reach me.'

'We'll stay in touch,' Valentino said.

Just then the baby woke.

'I'm going to call her Patty,' Yolanda said.

They said their good-byes and left the hospital. It was the end of a warm day, and as they walked to the Pontiac in the fading sunshine, Patty took off her coat and felt the sun warm her skin. Johnny sat behind the wheel, his arm in a plaster.

'Why don't I drive?' Patty said.

'I didn't think you knew how.'

'What, just because I'm a hitchhiker I don't know how to drive?'

'You didn't say where you wanted to go.'

'There are a few things I haven't said, Johnny.'

'Back there. You were going to tell me something.'

'There are different types of killer, Johnny. And not all of them are killers. We've been faced with the worst kind, the psychopaths who enjoy mutilating people, the men who profit from it and don't give a damn. Then you have those who don't know what they're doing, and those who are killing the killers.'

'What are you trying to tell me, Patty?'

'If you tell someone you did some things, things that on the outside look wrong, they don't understand, they don't know what events drove you to that place, but they're not the same as those things that men like Donald Lake do. If you're on the inside of those events maybe you understand.'

'You never did find Daisy.'

'I did. Daisy wasn't my sister, she's me. I'm called Daisy. My middle name is Patty. These days I call myself Patty Knight. I adopted my middle name some years ago to forget the events that happened to me. They're the reason I came back out here. Some people did some real bad things to me. Some of them were tied to the prostitution racket.'

'How do you know Alfred Bennett is dead?'

'Because I killed him. I killed Theodore first, then Ronny, then Renee, and finally him. Alfred lured me into meeting him, so he could rape me. I thought he was going to offer me a job. Then he bribed me to keep my mouth shut. When he found out I was pregnant he and Theodore raped me, then they aborted my baby with a coat hanger. Ronny and Renee held me down. Ronny was married to Alfred. Renee was his mistress and a sicker bitch you couldn't find if you searched for her. They were taking me out to the incinerator to get rid of me when I jumped out of the back of the van. I hitched a ride out of the area, went back to New York. I was in bad shape. I bled, I got an infection. I'll never have kids now.'

'Patty, that's terrible.'

'Yolanda said Marshall used to call her Renee, he was recreating his time with that bitch. I used your Jeep when I killed her and Ronny. You were sleeping. I didn't like hiding this from you, Johnny.'

'How did you find out where he was holding Yolanda?'

'I picked him up after I got away from Norman's ambush,

ain't that funny? His car had broken down. He wasn't dressed like Alfred, he was Marshall. I drove him to a truck, and he tried to rape me in the back of it to thank me for the ride. That's where I killed him. Then I ran out of gas and hitched a ride from Donald Lake.'

'You did the right thing,' Johnny said.

'In telling you this?'

'In killing them, Patty.'

'If I'd known how big the organisation was I don't think I would have come back.'

'Yeah, and I wouldn't have come out here for a story.'

'But you got one.'

'Oh, I got one all right.'

'And you got me.

'The best part of it.'

'You mean that, Johnny?'

'You think because of what you've told me I don't still think the same way of you? You were getting rid of men and women who should have ended up in their own incinerator. That area made us all kill. You have to kill out there to stay alive, but it doesn't mean we're murderers, not like them.'

'I also killed Sam Roche. I saw him sneaking into Natasha's house. He was trying to rape her. The night Red abducted me I had a Taser on me. He hadn't tied one of my hands tight enough, and I managed to give him a load of volts. I killed him in his house.'

'You saved your own life.'

'So where we gonna go, Johnny?'

'Wherever you want to.'

'I don't really have no particular direction no more.'

'I think I've seen enough of the frontier.'

'I want to go to a normal town where the cops aren't running rackets and supplying women as rape fodder.'

'What part of America would you be talking about?'

'Anywhere except where we've been, those four small towns.'

'OK, you're driving, Patty.'

They got out of the car, Johnny sat in the passenger seat, and Patty sat behind the wheel.

'Are you really OK with what I've told you, Johnny?'

'Sure.'

'And me not being able to have kids.'

'Why would it matter to me?'

She turned her brown eyes on him, and he began to melt. Then she started up the engine.

53.

10:00 p.m.

Patty filled up with gas, drove out of Tucson and back onto the highway. They found themselves passing Scarsdale again. After a few miles they saw Purity.

'You think they'll be safe coming back here?' Patty said.

'There's no one left who's looking for them.'

'That we know of.'

'Turn off. Let's have a look around.'

She entered the small town again and toured its silent streets.

'Place looks deserted,' she said.

'Valentino and Natasha said they were only coming back to pack and leave.'

Patty stopped outside The Morality Inn. Its sign had lost a hinge, and it swung in the breeze.

'Good-bye to Purity,' she said.

She drove out of the town.

'So how do we get out?' Patty said.

'Keep driving. Remember when we left the Morality Inn, you slept in the Jeep. I saw a blocked off section of highway. The house Donald Lake took you to occupies some land beyond it. They shut the highway to trap people and to hide him. And I think I've just figured out how we leave the area.'

They passed miles of familiar landscape.

'You think if Donald Lake hadn't ended up out here things would have been different?' Patty said.

'I don't know. Theodore and Alfred were running the racket for a long time, and they needed him. Roche and Norman got him out here to create organised sexual sadism with a profit involved.'

'They succeeded.'

'But they couldn't control Lake. His appetites surpassed their own, so they created the myth of the maniac trucker.'

'I never did thank you.'

'Why you stopping?'

Patty pulled over and kissed him deeply on the mouth.

'Think we can find a motel for the night?' she said. 'I have plans for you.'

'I hope my arm doesn't get in the way.'

'There's always the other hand.'

'You notice the landscape's changing?'

She looked out of the window. The highway was opening up, and she could see mountains.

'I didn't notice those before.'

'We need to turn off there,' Johnny said, pointing to a bend in the road.

She took the turn.

After a few miles they came to some traffic cones in front of a barrier. They got out and moved the cones.

'What now?' Patty said.

'We ram the barrier.'

They got back in the car, and Patty accelerated towards it under a deep blue night sky. The barrier arm buckled and broke, denting the front of the Pontiac. She drove on and got onto another section of highway. They passed a gas station and a diner.

'This is the way out,' Johnny said.

'You hungry?'

They went inside and sat together in a recess. They ate burgers and drank coffee. Afterwards Patty stood outside and smoked a cigarette. Its burning red tip looked like a firefly in the night air. Then they got back in the Pontiac. After a few miles they saw road signs and a town in the distance.

'You think that's civilisation?' Johnny said.

'I'm always hopeful. I ain't seen no truckers for a while.

'I don't think they use this route.'

'Johnny, promise me one thing. You write the story.'

'Oh, I will, it's the reason I went out there.'

'No regrets?'

'None at all. Look at what I'm taking back.'

'So where we going?'

'Come back to Ontario with me, Patty.'

'I think that's where the highway's headed.'

She drove on beneath a pale moon, her face softened in its light. And she and Johnny returned home.

Use this link to sign up for advance notice
of Richard Godwin's Next Book:
http://wildbluepress.com/AdvanceNotice

Word-of-mouth is critical to an author's long-term success.
If you appreciated this book please leave a review on the
Amazon sales page:
http://wbp.bz/shreviews

Coming to WildBlue Press and Investigation Discovery February 2016

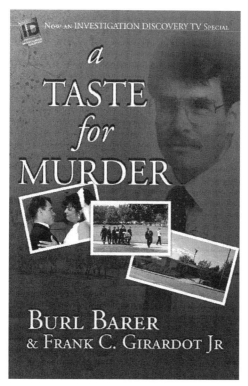

Now an INVESTIGATION DISCOVERY TV Special

a TASTE *for* MURDER

BURL BARER
& FRANK C. GIRARDOT JR

http://wbp.bz/atasteformurder
www.WildBluePress.com

A TASTE FOR MURDER

BY

BURL BARER AND FRANK GIRARDOT

PRE-ORDER YOUR COPY NOW FOR $2.99!

Frank Garcia, a much-loved counselor of troubled teens, lies dead on the bedroom floor. His wife and step-daughter are in shock, and so is the medical examiner when he performs the autopsy. Aside from being dead, Frank is in perfect health. Demanding to know the cause of her husband's death, Angie Garcia badgers the police, insisting that he was murdered. The cops attribute her assertions to overwhelming grief, but soon they too believe that Frank didn't die of natural causes. When the police enlist their number one suspect to help in the investigation, things spiral out of control until police are dealing with a daring plot to murder Angie's best friend and allegations of another homicide so evil and perverse that even seasoned L.A County Detectives are shocked beyond belief. Edgar Award winner Burl Barer teams with famed crime journalist Frank C. Girardot, Jr to bring you a true story so bizarre and disturbing that Investigation Discovery devoted a full hour to exploring this epic mystery - A TASTE FOR MURDER.

Read More About A TASTE FOR MURDER At:
http://wbp.bz/atasteformurder
www.WildBluePress.com

More True Crime You'll Love
From WildBlue Press.

Learn more at: http://wbp.bz/tc

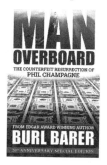

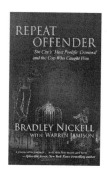

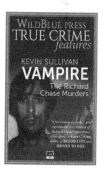

www.WildBluePress.com

More Mysteries/Thrillers You'll Love From WildBlue Press.

Learn more at: http://wbp.bz/cf

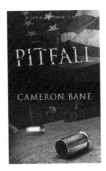 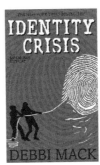 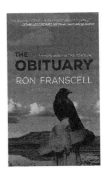

www.WildBluePress.com

Go to WildBluePress.com to sign up for our newsletter!

By subscribing to our newsletter you'll get *advance notice* of all new releases as well as notifications of all special offers. And you'll be registered for our monthly chance to win a **FREE collection of our eBooks and/or audio books** to some lucky fan who has posted an honest review of our one of our books/eBooks/audio books on Amazon, Itunes and GoodReads.

Let Someone Else Do The Reading.
Enjoy One Of Our Audiobooks

Learn more at: http://wbp.bz/audio

Please feel free to check out more True CRIME books
by our friends at

www.RJPARKERPUBLISHING.com

  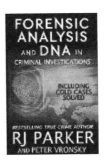

56316173R00146

Made in the USA
San Bernardino, CA
10 November 2017